WEATHER TO ORDER

A.L. SMITH

ISBN: 978-1-4834-5425-2 (sc)
ISBN: 978-1-4834-5426-9 (e)

Because of the dynamic nature of the Internet, any web addresses or links contained in this book may have changed since publication and may no longer be valid. The views expressed in this work are solely those of the author and do not necessarily reflect the views of the publisher, and the publisher hereby disclaims any responsibility for them.

Any people depicted in stock imagery provided by Thinkstock are models, and such images are being used for illustrative purposes only. Certain stock imagery © Thinkstock.

Lulu Publishing Services rev. date: 07/06/2016

WEATHER FORECAST

This is the third book of the series written in tribute to those 'wonders of Wythenshawe' who deliver themselves or their weather in pursuit of customer requirements.

'Making rain and other things is our business!' introduced readers to the crew of the Nimbus and provided an insight into their world of weather. 'A Cloud's Life' elaborated on their work and 'Weather to Order' continues to describe the climate they interfere with.

Fund raising in different forms, industrial espionage and TV drama work all figures in the working life of Wythenshawe's cloud machines along with the usual rain and other things. It's all part of life's rich pattern of weather.

New machines, new research, new crews, all point to a future for weather making or removing, as the case may be. Nothing stands still, not even a cloud, and the world waits to experience the fruits of man's attempts to harness the climate.

In a world full of regulation it is not surprising that this process is extended towards the heavens. The EU, in its infinite wisdom, has an eye on the sky and dreams of a cloud policy that will match its agricultural policy.

In a society which bestows awards like confetti, it should come as no surprise that the world of weather-making has joined in. It isn't televised or broadcast, but it does happen, once a year.

Rain, hail or snow, life can't go on without a touch of romance. Let's face it, even cloud crews are only human, although you may be tempted to think not when you are on the receiving end of a drenching.

DEDICATION

The vagaries of British weather never fail to amaze those on the receiving end of it and even the forecasters are caught out at times.

Whilst the weather is, generally, nothing to laugh about, that's exactly what we British tend to do; that's how we cope with it.

Talking about the weather is a typically British thing and this book is dedicated to all who engage in exactly that.

I hope this book gives you more weather to talk about.

# CONTENTS

Maps

PREFACE

Weather to Order
Background to the stories

By A.L.(Tony) Smith

From very small beginnings in 1985 the weather-making industry began and its clientele were very young. The industry has grown and its current clientele span a very wide age group from around the globe.

My first book – **Making rain and other things is our business!** – takes the reader from those early beginnings to the modern day hurly-burly of making rain and other things. My second - **A Cloud's Life** – continued the revelations. **Weather to Order** – illustrates both the history of weather-making and its progressive development.

Spending their final years in the 'Head in the Sky' rest home, retired cloud machine crews are able to describe the formation of the 'Cloud Corps' and the very first attempts at weather-making in an effort to thwart an enemy across the channel. Current crews are able to assist these brave ancestors by raising funds to keep a roof over their heads.

A combination of an interfering EU and unscrupulous entrepreneurs combine to create a headache for the work of Wythenshawe's established crews but that's just the way of things and the passage of time seems to ensure a natural equilibrium – nothing changes much in the end.

Development ensures that new cloud machines are able to perform a wider range of weather-making which is not always used in a legitimate fashion. The establishment of a weather-making research centre paves the way for an exciting future of predictable weather and all the advantages that may have. The new centre requires new machines and new crews, and new faces appear on the weather scene to join Cirrus Cumulus and his faithful engineer, Percival (Puffy) White, the central characters in these tales.

An established weather-making scenario would not be complete without its own annual awards and for the first time its workings are revealed.

Weather-making is a tight-knit world that normally keeps quiet about its work. This book provides the reader with a rare insight into the way rain, snow, hailstones and other things are sometimes the feature of 'Weather to Order', but be prepared for almost anything.

 **ACKNOWLEDGEMENTS**

As with my first two books, 'Making rain and other things is our business!' and 'A Cloud's Life', this latest addition could not have been created without the help of three particular people. My neighbour Helen cast an eye over my work looking for spelling, punctuation and other mistakes, and found plenty. Without her help I could never have got this far. Andy Cooper from Draw & Code Ltd has the ability to create superbly charismatic covers and he has succeeded in doing that for this publication. My friend Eddie drew two important illustrations for me and then drew a conclusion about my weather - making sanity. I am indebted to each of them but I do hope that if they intend visiting me, that they will remember, I don't like grapes.

INTRODUCTION

Weather to Order

By A.L.(Tony) Smith

Those of you who have read my books – 'Making Rain and Other Things Is Our Business'! and – 'A Cloud's Life' – will be well aware that a good deal of weather originates in Wythenshawe Weather Centre, care of its resident cloud machines. The crews of these machines form a tight community which is fostered by the Guild of Cloud-Owners, and their welfare extends into retirement through the Guild's rest home – 'The Head in the Sky' – situated in Grange-over-Sands.

This latest edition in the series – 'Weather to Order' – traces the roots of man-made weather-making through the reminiscing of the residents of 'The Head in the Sky'. Wartime and the formation of the 'Cloud Corps' came as a complete surprise to the central figures of the stories – Cirrus Cumulus and Percival (Puffy) White, but things had come a long way since 1945.

Renovation of the rest home demanded considerable cash, and fund-raising became the order of the day for cloud machine owners. Using their extensive imagination, ingenuity and creativity, they raised the money by conducting events such as:'guess how long it will drizzle for', a 'who is the prettiest cloud contest', 'guess how many of us are up here, mixed up with nature's mob' - and others.

As in most walks of life, the EU is having its impact and weather-making is no exception. New EU proposals included: 'banning rain on Sundays', 'parking fees for hovering clouds', 'imposition of cloud speed limits' and 'the fitting of tachographs'. They were all met with derision.

Whilst TV Drama work and Industrial Sabotage were all in a day's weather-making, the notion of guaranteeing good weather was a new concept in its infancy, but it commanded big interest from a number of event organisers.

In the world of weather, time doesn't stand still and the latest machines from manufacturers Black, Black & Blakemore's were able to provide a wider variety of inclement conditions that increased Wythenshawe's extensive repertoire of weather to order.

Research is an ongoing thing and the world of weather is not to be excluded. The creation of a new Research Centre had big implications for the future, but, for the present, new crews would be required to operate new machines and training for the role was a pre-requisite.

There is nothing better than the giving of awards to maintain morale, and the Guild of Cloud-Owners recognised this and implemented their own annual prize giving ceremony to ensure the future of weather-making to order.

The stories' central figures are never far from politics or girls, although girls, on the whole, got more attention than politics. Passion and politics may seem strange bedfellows but if you spend most of your life with your head in the clouds, nothing would be considered strange!

 # HOW IT USED TO BE

Visiting old friends

The Guild of Cloud-Owners ran a rest home in Grange-over-Sands called 'The Head in the Sky" although those who were spending their last days there were more inclined to call it 'The Halfway House'. There are full-time and temporary residents, all with a background of service either operating, servicing or administering cloud machines. By and large they were a cheerful lot hell-bent on enjoying their stay.

The rest home was in an old mansion house that currently accommodated twenty-five residents of whom fifteen were full time. A house staff of caring care workers and a resident nurse doted on the retired cloud-workers and there was always a pleasant atmosphere about the place. Each resident has a self-contained apartment and shares a plush dining room and lounge which has a bar that is decorated with cloud mementos from a very coloured past.

'The Head in the Sky' is situated on a hill to the north of Grange-over-Sands with a commanding view across Morecambe Bay and is in its own grounds. It is a most attractive place. A week's stay here was eagerly sought after by the current team operating out of Wythenshawe Weather Centre and it was a great opportunity to connect with their illustrious past. The full-time residents were always delighted by their temporary companions' visits for it gave them the chance to talk clouds again.

Cirrus and his faithful engineer Percival White, Puffy to his friends, made one of their regular visits to the 'Head in the Sky' rest home to spend a little time with Alf Fisher. Alf had been a close friend of Cirrus's father when he was alive and had been a resident in the Grange-over-Sands Home for a number of years. Alf always looked forward to a visit from the crew of the cloud machine Nimbus.

"Nice to see you two boys," said Alf as he greeted Cirrus and Puffy.

"Meet my pals, George and Fred."

They all shook hands and exchanged pleasantries and when the tea and cakes arrived the fivesome were ready to engage in a full-blown cloud conversation.

"Tell us what you have been up to since I last saw you'" said Alf.

Stories of the Nimbus fighting fires, delivering spies, guiding a lost ship and posing for calendar photos fascinated the trio of residents who all wished it had been themselves doing it. What they were less likely to have had the inclination to be involved with concerned the Nimbus crashing or being hit by a missile, not to mention being frozen into a huge lump of cloud ice, but it was all very interesting to listen to.

"I believe you did a course recently at Bishops Court Training Centre Cirrus."

Cirrus, with the aid of Puffy, gave the happy trio the rundown on their participation on the course covering emergency procedures.

A good hour or so had passed by and Cirrus thought to himself that the conversation had all been one sided until now and he was anxious to give the veterans the chance to tell some of their stories.

Alf was the first to seize the chance.

"Me and your grandfather, Cirrus, we both joined up at the same time in October 1940. We joined the Royal Air Force to work on aircraft and they sent us to Padgate for square-bashing. Well, we survived that and we both got sent to Blackpool. The RAF had set up a Technical Training School in the town and a few of the big stores were turned into classrooms and workshops and me and your grandfather trained to be aircraft airframe fitters."

"What happened after you had finished your training?" asked Puffy.

"We were lucky, they posted us both to RAF Hendon near London and we were both attached to a squadron that used Lysander aircraft to help calibrate some of the stuff the anti-aircraft gunners used. That was not such a bad posting but then they sent us to a place called Shobdon.

That was in 1942 and that was a bit of a dump. We were attached to an anti-aircraft co-operation unit there. The blokes on the unit were great but your grandfather and me wanted something a bit more glamorous, so we both started to look for something else to have a go at and that's when we found out the RAF was forming up 'The Cloud Corps'. Well, we both jumped at it and applied. We got interviewed in Gloucester but that's when me and your grandfather went separate ways. Your grandfather got posted to India and I got accepted into The Cloud Corps."

"I never realised there was such a thing as 'The Cloud Corps'" announced Cirrus.

"It was all kept hush-hush in them days but George here and Fred, they were all in it an all." Alf then continued, "I got sent to Cardington to train as a pilot on the early cloud machines and that's when us three first met. We all qualified in 1943 and then we all got moved to Wythenshawe which was just opening up at that time."

"So that explains the purpose of the plaque in the Weather Centre. I've often wondered about it. 'The Cloud Corps', well that is interesting'" said Puffy.

"Everything was so new then and it took a long time for us to get ready for what the Air Ministry had in mind for us," continued Alf and then George interrupted.

"When I met Alf in Cardington I had just been posted there. I didn't volunteer, I had a good job in the stores at Aston Down, a real cushy number but my Flight Sergeant thought I was having it too easy so he filled the form in for me."

"What about you Fred, how did you get involved with this cloud mob?"

"My story was a bit different from the other two. In 1942 I was stationed at RAF Duxford which was a fighter station then, and I was a mechanic. I got quite attached to a WAAF in the station headquarters. A real good looker she was too, tall, slim and she wobbled in all the right places. Anyway, she got posted to Cardington and the only way I could get to see her again was by getting posted there too, so I did and the next thing you know I was getting air sick in a bloomin cloud machine. What made it worse was that I got posted to Wythenshawe."

"What happened to the WAAF?"

"Oh, she fell for a Yank and went to live in Texas after the war. I soon got another though and she was a corker an all."

There was plenty spirit about this lot thought Cirrus.

Much simpler cloud machines

"Who manufactured those wartime cloud machines, Alf?"

"It was Black, Black & Blackemore's in deeper Salford. They are the only manufacturers in the business. They built all the original machines and they have carried on ever since."

"What did those early cloud machines look like?" asked Cirrus.

"They had the same bullet-shaped fuselage as the present ones but in them days they had wings and a fin, just like real aeroplanes," replied Alf.

"Describe them for me, Alf."

"Well, for a start, you had to take a short ladder with you to get in them. The door was on the port side as it is now but it was padlocked on the outside when they were not being used and you needed a key for it. On the inside of the door there was a sliding bolt to keep it closed in flight. There were no washing facilities, not even a loo, just a pee tube. We didn't have a galley either; you just took enough sandwiches and flasks of tea or coffee to keep you going. It was all a bit crude compared with today."

"How were those wartime machines powered?" asked Puffy.

"They had an aero engine and propeller on the front to give forward propulsion and it was linked to a set of rotors on the top of the craft to give extra lift at the low speeds that clouds fly at and we couldn't hover like you do now, we just flew very slowly. You couldn't ascend or descend vertically; you did that ever so gradually like an aircraft but slower."

"How did you get off the ground then?"

"You took off like any aeroplane does but much slower. We had to operate from prepared airfields, not like it is now. You can land or take off anywhere, like a helicopter, but with our primitive jobs we could only use aerodromes."

At this point Fred moved in on the conversation.

"Sometimes it was really funny. You got airborne an went off an found some water to atomise, just like you do now, an make a cloud to use on Hitler's mob an then come home an land. You were supposed to get rid of all your cloud before comin home but I remember a few of the boys comin back with a bit left an it was real funny to watch a cloud come in an land an taxi in to its dispersal an the maintenance lads would go mad cos they had to get rid of it an they usually got soaked in the process. You can imagine it." And they could.

Alf picked up where he had left off. "Our machines had a fixed undercarriage and for take off we would taxi out from our dispersal to the end of the runway, turn into the wind, line up with the centre line, open the throttle wide and off you would go. We got airborne at a very slow speed and climbed away slowly."

"So it was like piloting an aircraft then?"

"Yes it was."

"How could you see where you were going? Did you have a TV camera in those days?"

"That's a good question. No we had no TV then."

Alf continued, "The things that belched the cloud out when we had atomised water…"

Before he could get any further, Cirrus broke in.

"Do you mean the dispensers?"

"That's right, the dispensers, well they were all placed on the sides of the fuselage towards the back end and that resulted in a cloud which was almost completely behind us. About the first third of the craft actually stuck out from the cloud and so we could see everything through our cockpit window."

"What about the Germans, couldn't they see you?"

"Once they worked out what was going on they did start looking for us but they only cottoned on late in the war and by then we had learned how to hide amongst the real stuff and that foxed them."

George butted in at this point. "That's right but the Germans did shoot a couple of our lads down before the war's end."

"I think I have seen their names on the memorial at Wythenshawe," remarked Cirrus.

George continued, "The machines had no parachutes fitted either in them days and although the crew had them there was little chance of baling out. They would have to move out of the cockpit and struggle down the corridor to the exit door and you could imagine how difficult

5

that would be when the machine was tumbling and twisting on its journey back down to earth."

Cirrus just looked at Puffy. The prospect of surviving in those conditions suddenly hit home.

"How did you find your way about in those days? How did you navigate? Did you have a Plan Position Indicator like we have in our machines?"

"No we didn't have a PPI. Navigation was all done with the mark one eyeball, a map and compass and a stopwatch. It was as simple as that and we got lost frequently, especially in the dark."

It was time for a breather and fortunately a tray of refreshments arrived and all five tucked in, but it wasn't going to be the end of the conversation. Cirrus and Puffy were both fascinated by the experiences of these former RAF Cloud Corps pilots. There was a lot more to learn from them and the old guys loved the opportunity to share their experiences.

What could the old machines do?

"Tell me more about your RAF cloud machines Alf," requested Cirrus.

"What do you want to know?"

"What kind of clouds could you make?"

"Only one! We could only make Cumberland Greys. Clouds like Westmorland Whites and Manchester Blacks were not even dreamed about at that stage of the war."

"What kind of rain could you make?"

"Well it was all wet stuff, what other kind is there?"

"I mean drizzle, light rain, downpours, that kind of thing."

"Oh, I see what you mean now. The first machines we had could do steady drizzle, light rain, heavy rain or a short downpour. Later models allowed us to do all those things in an intermittent mode as well."

"How long could you rain for?"

"That depended on the size of cloud we made. We had no water tanks so we couldn't store any and we had no refrigerators or sublimator so we couldn't freeze any water and then turn it into cloud, so in the end it all depended on the size of cloud we made. With the biggest Cumberland Grey we could make, we could drizzle for a solid hour but light rain or heavy rain would last a bit less and if it was a downpour it would only last for fifteen minutes. Later machines could do a deluge but that would only last ten minutes."

"What about other weather? Could you do anything else like thunder, snow, that kind of thing?"

"Blimey, you do want to know a lot of things! Well, we didn't have the know-how of making thunder or lightning, all that came well after the war and as far as snow or hailstones are concerned, well even you with your latest up-market machines can't do that."

"That's true but the manufacturers in deeper Salford are working on it," replied Cirrus.

"What about cloud colouring, could you do that?"

"No, no, nothing like that. All our clouds were grey, a very dull grey, that's all we could do."

Development

Five happy comrades, each with their heads happily in the clouds, continued to talk about all things connected with weather making and the development of cloud machines. Things had come along way since World War Two and Salford had continued to be the centre of both research and production through manufacturer Black, Black & Blackemore's.

As soon as the Second World War had ended, the RAF lost interest in using cloud machines. The Cloud Corps was disbanded in 1946. In the next four or more years there was little in the way of development and Salford's centre of cloud excellence almost went bust. The setting up of Wythenshawe Weather Centre by the Meteorological Office saved it. The buildings had previously been the headquarters of the RAF Cloud Corps and had been purpose built to house the machines of that time. With a future in store, Black, Black & Blackemore's began to invest in new ideas.

In the 1950s saddle shaped water tanks were added to the sides of the cloud machines increasing the duration of time they could rain. A proper toilet was installed along with washing facilities and these made a big difference to the crews who could be called upon to spend several days at a time flying and making weather. During the same decade Identification Beacons, ID for short, were installed. They were not much direct use to the crews on board at this time but for the radar people down below and on the aircraft of the period; they were most useful for they identified the blip that represented them on a radar display.

The 1960s had seen the most radical and far reaching developments take place. First came the fan duct motor that revolutionised cloud machines. Up until this point the machines had an aero engine and propeller on the front of them and this was linked to a set of rotor blades on top, but this changed dramatically. The aero engine, propeller and rotor blades all disappeared. Replacing them were four fan duct motors, two on each side of the craft. These motors were mounted on a ball joint which permitted them to be turned to the left and to the right as well as up and down. They not only turned the cloud machines, they also made them ascend and descend and in doing so they made the crafts wings and fin redundant. The machines could now be made to hover and there were all kinds of interesting possibilities to explore with this ability. It was a massive step forward. Second, in the same decade great improvements inTelevision technologies were taking place and the cloud machines greatly benefitted. A rotatable periscope was mounted on the top of the cloud machines and it housed a TV camera with an infra-red facility allowing it to see in the dark and, equally as important, through its own cloud. To take advantage of this all round vision a pop-up TV screen was mounted on the flight deck giving the crew maximum visual awareness of everything around them. With the TV camera installed there was no reason for the machines to have their nose stuck out from the front of the cloud which was a giveaway for any potential enemy and hence the cloud dispensers mounted on the machines were redistributed around the sides to ensure that it was fully immersed in any cloud it made. It would now be invisible to the world. As if all this was not enough, Black, Black & Blackemore's perfected the technique of making other types of clouds, and Westmorland Whites and Manchester Blacks were added to the current Cumberland Greys to provide a useful repertoire.

In the 1970s emergency parachutes were installed in a housing on top of the machines. These could be deployed if there was a loss of power and that would give the crew a better chance of survival. A retractable undercarriage was also installed during this decade but this was more of a controversy since many wondered about its relevance and these days it is left lowered almost all the time. The really important advance in this decade concerned navigation. A device called a Soakometer was developed which was an early form of navigation aid or navaid. The first four letters stood for 'Search, Overland, Absorb and Karry. Different water sources at that time had been allocated a star rating and represented different levels of quality. The object of the Soakometer was to automatically fly a cloud machine to any desired water source by punching into a keyboard the latitude and longitude of its position and on arrival it would atomise or absorb the water and create a cloud ready for delivery. The Absorb feature had long been discontinued and the Soakometer, these days, was simply used as a navigation aid or navaid. The atomising of water is still, of course, a central part of a cloud machine but its operation is controlled from the Flight Engineer's work station and not the flight-deck-mounted Soakometer. A second navigation aid appeared at this time in the form of a Plan Position Indicator or PPI for short. This device consisted of a circular TV screen mounted on the top of a tubular column to the left of the pilot's seat so that it was easily observable. A green line extended from the centre of the screen to its outer edge and it rotated through 360°. The ground below the cloud was clearly shown in map-like form, day or night. Other aircraft or cloud machines within a radius of fifty miles could also be observed in the form of permanent blips and their position relative to your own could be clearly seen. It was at this time that the advantage of having an ID Beacon became evident. The beacons permitted identification details to be displayed alongside each blip which was most helpful for air traffic controllers and the military if there was any danger of foreign intervention in the air space in question.

The 1980s brought less in the way of ground breaking ideas but there were still some developments. Cloud machines got a galley and a winch was fitted, but like the retractable undercarriage there were those that wondered why. The real development of this decade was the installation of refrigerators and sublimators. The refrigerators allowed some of the atomised water to be stored on board as ice and the sublimators enabled the ice to be turned back into cloud vapour as required. This extended the duration of rain making and especially if a heavy downpour or deluge had been ordered. Some asked why more water tanks could not have been used instead of refrigerators. The fact is that Black, Black & Blackemore's had been working on giving the cloud machines the ability to make hailstones, snow and slush for some time and refrigerators had been part of that plan, but to date they had not succeeded.

During the 1990s an automatically opening door and deployable access ladder were installed and both could be activated by pushing a button on the outside of the craft and there was another on the inside. For security purposes a keyboard was mounted on the outside of the craft into which a security code was punched before the outside button would work but this could be disabled if needed and that was the case when machines were kept in Wythenshawe Weather Centre's huge hangar to comply with Health & Safety regulations. It was during this decade that a drop-down double bunk was installed which was welcomed by the crews. If you had to be aboard for several days and nights the crew needed somewhere to get their heads down. Finally, this was the decade when mobile phones reached the world of clouds and a suitable antenna was fixed on the stern of each machine.

The last decade, the 2000s, had seen its own projects in the Salford cloud machine works come to fruition. Installation of a mixer and luminance control gave each machine the incredible ability to make clouds of different colours and of different levels of luminosity. Whilst this does not accurately replicate nature it is, nevertheless, a stunning feature when used in certain situations. A thunder player and loudspeakers linked into a lightning creating Van-de-Graaf generator was also installed during this decade. This was a time when the idea of accurate cloud formation flying was being trialled and the installation of a Vertical Separation Indicator or VSI for short, proved very useful in ensuring that each cloud was at the same altitude. The last innovation of the decade was the Global Positioning System which enabled the crew to check its exact latitude and longitude using orbiting satellites. This was useful as a back up if other navigation aids failed.

Most recently, a Morse key had been installed and linked to the luminance control. These versatile cloud machines now had the ability to switch a coloured cloud on and off rapidly, indeed for those conversant with Morse code, messages could be received from a winking cloud. As for the future, well, Black, Black & Blackemore's were still working on the idea of making hailstones, snow and slush.

"Now you must have your tea with us before you go," said Alf and the five of them retired to the dining room.

Wartime reminiscing

"What sort of things did you do during the War?" asked Cirrus.

Alf responded first. "We used to go out with the Atlantic convoys to spot German submarines. That was an important job. America was our lifeline for food and military supplies during the War and it was essential to ensure that our ships could sail back and forth to the USA safely. The Germans tried to stop us by sinking our ships. To try and preserve the link we sent our ships in large groups at a time called convoys and each one had an escort of Navy boats to protect them but they had a difficult job on their hands. The RAF helped by sending out long range patrol aircraft to try and spot the submarines and to sink them, but the aircraft had a limited range and as the convoys got further into the Atlantic they could only stay on station for a short time. The Navy also used small aircraft carriers called escort carriers to try and protect the convoys but it was still a difficult job. Anyway, the Admiralty requested that the Cloud Corps be commandeered to assist and that's where we came in."

"You mean, you went out over the Atlantic with the convoys?"

"That's right, that's what we did and it was bloody boring most of the time. We spent hours and hours of daylight looking out for those German submarines."

"What did you do if you spotted one?" asked Puffy.

"We had a radio transmitter and we just called up one of the Navy escort boats and left it to them."

"What did you do when it was dark?"

"Bugger all! We couldn't see anything so we just flew on through the night at the same speed as the convoy and on the same heading and hoped that when the dawn broke it would still be down below us. On a moonlit night we could see the ships on the surface of the ocean, but on most nights it was just too dark to see anything and on many an occasion when dawn broke there was no convoy in sight, we just lost it. During the night if the wind strength and direction changed it could blow us away from the convoy and we wouldn't know it was happening."

"So what did you do then?"

We had to start and search for it and sometimes we never found it again and had to head for home."

"Could the Germans not tell that you were not real clouds? Could they not see part of your cloud machines sticking out from your Cumberland Greys?"

"We had strict instructions not to fly lower than 5000 feet because at that height they couldn't tell, but that did of course limit our usefulness. Often the natural cloud base would be much lower than 5000 feet. If that was the case and there was a strong suspicion that German submarines were about, the instruction was ignored."

"How did you go on for food and drink if you were airborne for weeks at a time?"

"All our food was pre-prepared and specially wrapped to keep it from going off but it was all cold stuff. We had a few flasks of hot drinks and an urn full of cold water. We took tea and coffee and sugar and powdered milk and a small spirit stove to boil the water. It was a bit risky using the stove; there was always the danger of it falling over if we flew through some turbulence."

"And what did you do for a loo?"

"We took a chemical loo on board with us. I think it was called an Elsan. It was all a bit primitive but we had to try and help our convoys."

The human fascination with all things morbid then raised its head with Cirrus enquiring about our cloud losses at this time.

"Oh we had our share of them all right. I remember poor old Jimmy Windfall. He was on patrol when an RAF Liberator aircraft mistook him for a real cloud and flew straight through him and collided with his machine. Well that was the end of poor old Jimmy; he fell out of the sky and straight into the freezing drink."

George butted in at this point to relate the tale of Oscar Thompson.

"Oscar was making a brew when his cloud flew into some turbulence and the stove fell over and set fire to his machine. He didn't have a fire extinguisher so he had to put it out with the chemical loo. He emptied its contents on the flames and the fire went out, but his machine stank until he got back home a week later and there was nowhere that they could go when nature called for all that time and the stench got worse."

There seemed to be something of a competition at this point for who could relate the strangest incident but the final tale fell to Fred who described how one of his colleagues simply disappeared overnight. He had been following the convoy until darkness fell one night but the next day he had just simply vanished. Now how could anyone search for a lost cloud in the middle of the Atlantic? They didn't have ID beacons then. The only way a convoy Captain could tell that he still had his protective cloud cover was by having a radio check at intervals but nothing was ever heard from the missing cloud, although rumour had it that its crew were spotted some years later in Brazil.

The topic then returned to the subject of spotting submarines.

"Oh yes, we did see some and we passed the information to the convoy leader and they went after them. In fact, we saw one or two being attacked but it was a long time ago."

"Do you remember us looking out for V1 flying bombs Alf?" enquired George.

"Yes I do but you tell them about it George." And so George began. "The Germans had designed and built these flying bombs called V1's: they were an early form of guided missile and they were launching them and targeting them at England. We didn't know where the launch sites were exactly although we had a fair idea that they were largely on the French and Belgian coasts. The Cloud Corps were sent to spot for them and we would take our Cumberland Greys across the channel and loiter overland and wait till they broke cover and fired one. When we had spotted one being fired we would radio back the co-ordinates of its location and then the RAF boys would do the rest. I remember hearing about one of our guys who saw the Germans break cover in one location and readied a V1 to fire and when he came to radio the information back he discovered that his radio was not working. He felt pretty useless but decided that he would have a go at thwarting the efforts of the enemy firing their V1 on England. He descended onto the launch area blanking out the rest of the world from its firing party thinking that that would be enough to prevent the launch from going ahead but it didn't. The Germans didn't need good visibility to launch their unmanned flying bomb and they launched straight into the cloud. Fortunately, it rocketed through the cloud and exited it just over the top of the cloud machine. The crew were a bit startled but not hurt and they left the scene as fast as they could."

Now it was the turn of Fred to do some wartime reminiscing and he related as to how he was once tasked to fly out to France during a very hot and dry period to give the Army some relief. He had to fly to a precise location where a large number of grimy soldiers had gathered and then he had to fly around them in circles until the troops realised that they had a cloud saviour overhead, at which point they all stripped off. Fred went on to describe what he saw but it isn't printable, save to say that amongst other things there were several hundred naked allied troop backsides on full display below them and it was time to rain. A full hour of light drizzle proved exquisite to the troops who had not had the chance to get a shower for over a month and they loved the experience of sharing one with all their soldier colleagues. They were, however, slightly displeased when they found that the drizzle had soaked their mud-caked uniforms that they had been so keen to take off a little earlier. It's rare for anyone to witness several hundred naked soldiers playing for time whilst their kit had the chance to dry out and they couldn't preserve their dignity. The locals came to see what all the excitement was about and found plenty of it.

It had been great listening to these wonderful stories from these great guys but Cirrus and his faithful engineer Puffy White couldn't stay for ever. With great sadness they bade farewell to the three veterans and left with a firm promise to return in the not too distant future. As they drove out of the grounds of 'The Head in the Sky' rest home, they gave a final wave of farewell and set off on the return journey to their home in Slaidburn. The journey was a quiet one as each of them was engrossed in thought about how things used to be.

 **AN APPEAL**

Funds are needed

Prudence McWhirter had been in charge of 'The Head in the Sky' rest home at Grange-over-Sands for many years and she was considered both efficient and caring. No-one had a bad word for her and she was held in high esteem by both the residents and 'The Guild of Cloud-Owners'. The day-to-day running costs of the home were borne by the Guild but repairs and improvements were financed by any means that Prudence could organise and this tended to be the most difficult part of her job. Currently her greatest worry was the state of the home's roof; it was badly in need of attention.

Local firm 'Wright's Roofers' were called in to investigate and confirm what needed doing and how much it would cost. Wright's were a local family firm with a good reputation and they had done a considerable amount of work on 'The Head in the Sky' over the years. The inspection was thorough but the results were not so heart-warming. The roof timbers were in a bad state and needed replacing and that meant taking off the whole of the roof and completely replacing it. The only consolation was that it could be done in stages so there would be no need to temporarily close the place, which was a relief. The cost, however, was enormous and ran into a couple of hundred thousand pounds.

Prudence approached 'The Guild of Cloud Owners' to help with the funding but their response was a little disappointing. The Guild could not directly fund the job but promised to try and raise what funds it could.

Basically, it was up to Prudence to find the finance required, not the Guild. She was well aware of the agreements made some years past but it was not helpful being reminded.

The process of raising funds began with applying for grants. Grant application is like trying to find your way through a maze, thought Prudence but she did her very best. The Local Authority was approached and many applications made to both local and national charities, but it was all so time consuming and answering all the questions on the various forms was a nightmare, in fact, she was reaching the conclusion that all the hurdles presented by the forms was symptomatic of a deterrent to applicants. In spite of all this, something in the region of a quarter of the money required was obtained through grants.

With the agreement of the residents it was decided to hold an open day at 'The Head in the Sky' and to invite as many dignitaries and business people as possible to come along and see the facilities and to encourage them to make donations to help keep the place going. The old building was splendid and the grounds most attractive and the setting was an ideal one in which to hold an open air buffet and so it was done. An entrance fee was charged for those not invited and a raffle was held using prizes donated from businesses in Grange-over-Sands. The event was a great success and several substantial donations helped to fill the coffers. A new roof was getting a bit nearer.

With just about a half of the necessary funds in the bag, Prudence was running out of ideas when one of the residents suggested she made an appeal to Wythenshawe Weather Centre. After careful deliberation she decided that she would do this and it wasn't long before the appeal appeared on the desk of the Centre's Superintendant, Mr I.N.Spite C.D.M.

An Appeal on behalf of the Cloud Crew Welfare Home

The Head in the Sky

Grange-over-Sands

**Do you know where you will be when you retire or
if you are disabled as a result of your work?**

The 'Head in the Sky' at Grange-over- Sands exists to provide
cloud machine crew members with a safe haven when things
have gone wrong. It is a place where people with something
in common can spend their time in pleasant company
and in a splendid setting to while away their time.

The home was set up by 'The Guild of Cloud Owners' to provide
for its members and The Guild funds the day-to-day running costs.

Currently the home is in need of a new
roof which will cost £200,000.

Grants and other fundraising activities
have raised half of that amount.

This is an appeal to all of you at Wythenshawe
Weather Centre for your help.

Can you help the home and its residents, both current
and future, by either raising funds and/or making
suggestions as to how this can be achieved?

Remember, raising the roof is the target!

Prudence McWhirter
Head of Care
The Head in the Sky
Grange-over-Sands

Mr Spite was most sympathetic when he had read the appeal and after
thinking about the condition of the roof he made a couple of decisions.
First, he decided to declare a cloud avoidance area around Grange-over-
Sands until the roof job was completed. And second, he would call a
meeting of the crews that operated from Wythenshawe Weather Centre
to discuss in detail what could be done. When all was said and done,
fund raising was not something new to them. He could still remember the
fund-raising they had done to pay for the electricity bill associated with

the rescue mission to find Lucy Windrush. As far as the cloud avoidance area was concerned, he realised that this would only be of limited value, since he had no control over nature's rain- delivering jobs and there were always plenty of them. Nevertheless, it was a case of every little bit helps.

Word gets around

Cirrus Cumulus had just finished reading the Daily Gloom in his Slaidburn home and was about to embark on his ritual 'what should the country be doing' thought process that always followed his newspaper reading session, when Puffy came in to the lounge with the latest post. Scanning through the various envelopes, he decided to look first at the one which had arrived from Wythenshawe Weather Centre.

"Hey Puffy, just come in here will you?"

Puffy stepped into the lounge fully expecting to hear his Captain's latest ideas about how the country should be run, which always happened after he had been reading the Daily Gloom, and hence he was taken by surprise as Cirrus began by asking, "Did you notice the roof of 'The Head in the Sky' when we were recently there?"

"Not in particular skipper, why?"

"Well, they have made an appeal to Wythenshawe Weather Centre for funds to get a new roof. There's a meeting being held next Wednesday. What a coincidence that we were only there a couple of weeks ago! Put it in our diary Puffy. We'd better attend that one."

"Aye, aye skipper," said Puffy, who then carried on with his chores whilst feeling a sense of relief that he had not been subjected to one of his skipper's political ear bashings.

On arrival at Wythenshawe it was pretty obvious that the appeal had struck a chord; nearly every cloud owner operating a machine out of the Centre appeared to have made the effort to attend. There were many small groups of individuals busy making re-acquaintances with old friends, and Cirrus and Puffy were not left out when they spotted Abigail Windrush and Carol Aspinall, the two women in their lives. This had all the makings of a pleasant evening. Perhaps they could all retire to The Silver Lining Club when the meeting was over.

Everybody was ushered into the conference hall and told to sit down. Then there was a wait and the noise level started to rise as conversations struck up between cloud crews. The Superintendant, Mr Spite C.D.M., strode into the hall and silence fell. Mr Spite commanded considerable respect. In fact this meeting was down to his initiative and the work of his secretary who everyone called Goldilocks. Mr Spite began;

"Thank you all for attending this meeting. It is indeed very rare that we all come together like this but it is in a good cause. As you all know, 'The Guild of Cloud Owners' run a rest home just for us at Grange-over-Sands and it does a splendid job for its residents, but for one reason or another it has fallen on hard times. The Head Care Worker, Prudence McWhirter is desperately trying to raise funds to get a new roof fitted. She has raised a half of what is needed and is now appealing to us for help and suggestions. I feel confident that you will all rise to this worthy challenge."

A general murmur of approval went around the hall, for 'The Halfway House', as it was known to everybody here, was a much valued facility. In the line of cloud making you never knew when you might need it. It all went quiet again as Mr Spite was about to speak again.

"I have a couple of ideas to discuss with you and then we can throw the meeting open for suggestions. First, I wonder if you would consider having a regular monthly payment taken out of your salaries."

This idea was not widely accepted, mostly due to the fact that, as someone pointed out, no-one present gets a regular salary; they all got paid a fee for each weather job they performed.

"Well that neatly brings me to my second idea which is, would you consider donating the fee for one of your jobs to the home?"

This idea got quite a hostile response. Many of those present highlighted how difficult it was to make a living out of making weather, especially in a place like the UK which had plenty already. Some were just about coping financially and the prospect of completing a job for nothing was simply not acceptable. In the end, after much debate, it was agreed that one percent of the income from each job they did would be donated towards the rest home and that was of some relief to Mr Spite.

The meeting was thrown open to ideas but they didn't come thick and fast and unique ideas were absent in the early part of the discussion. The usual fundraising activities raised their heads such as individual members participating in sponsored 'slims' which may have been of medical benefit looking at some of those present. Raffles, of course, were mentioned by many. Not quite so usual was the suggestion of producing scratch cards but not with the names of football clubs on them but the names of cloud machines instead, and whichever machine was picked as the winner the owner would provide a cash prize. The cash prize bit was hotly contended and after a somewhat heated exchange the prize was changed to a joy ride in the winning machine.

The meeting then went on to explore other ways in which funds could be acquired and a list of five events that could be planned and put into practice was created. The details of each took some time to agree as did the dates and venues, but the biggest difficulty came when a committee had to be formed whose duty it would be to organise these five events. The cloud owners were just so typical of society at large, full of ideas for someone else to carry out, but a committee was formed although it has to be said that some of the members did not appear too enthusiastic.

Drizzle for funds

Wally Lenticular aboard the Discovery agreed to perform the first fundraising event which was to be staged at several holiday resorts on the west coast stretching from Morecambe to Rhyl. Morecambe would be the venue for Wally's inaugural activity. A tent was erected on the promenade where holiday makers could have a flutter by guessing how long it would drizzle for, starting at a specific time. The winner would receive a prize of £100. Entry cost £1 and candidates had to write on a form the exact time in hours, minutes and seconds they thought it would last and, finally, give their contact details. Taking a day off from weather-making, Abigail Windrush agreed to time the drizzle when it happened.

On a day when there was not a cloud in the sky, it was hard to convince people that it would start drizzling at exactly 3-00pm and a number of accusations were made that the whole thing was nothing but a con trick. Whilst some chose to abuse Abigail, others thought it was a huge laugh especially when they read that the funds were to go to a rest home for cloud machine crews. Who ever heard of such a thing – cloud machines – they must be barmy! In spite of all the doubt and suspicion surrounding the impending drizzle, there was a steady flow of contributions and it was not long before the prize money of £100 had been established. The event was now into profit.

Lunch time arrived and Morecambe beach was seeing a steady flow of sunbathers gathering to enjoy the rare treat of good weather. Deck chairs and towels marked family encampments as groups of all ages prepared for the midday sun. Cameras clicked, or at least the old ones did and new castles were constructed that would not withstand the passage of tide. Each castle tower proudly displayed a miniature flag as the proud builders worked away at making the ramparts ever bigger. Slim females in bikinis spread out on towels to turn white skin into slightly less white but mostly pink and in worse cases, red. Less slim females tested the durability of deck chairs and dished out sandwiches with a little sand as an extra. As for the males, well the younger ones were busy working on castles whilst those a bit older were bikini spotting. The much older males took it all in their sleep which was aided and abetted by a newspaper. What everyone had in common however was a firm conviction that it was not going to drizzle at 3-00pm.

Wally had arrived at Wythenshawe Weather Centre the day before with his Flight Engineer Bert Drummond. They spent the afternoon checking over their cloud machine, the Discovery, in Wythenshawe's huge hangar before gathering together the provisions they would need to keep them going. Then it was a long wait until it got dark at which point they started the Discovery's four fan duct motors and taxied out of the hangar and into the darkness of the outside World. A few instrument checks and a call for clearance to take off to Wythenshawe Control and they ascended vertically into the night sky and didn't stop until reaching five thousand feet.

The Discovery then headed west toward the Irish Sea. All this was being done in the night to comply with the regulations laid down in the Cloud Machine Rules of Operation Manual which clearly states that cloud machines must never be identifiable by the general public, and right now the Discovery was naked and would remain so until a cloud was created around it. Currently, thousands of lights below the Discovery were clearly observable through the cockpit window but that would not be for long. When it was in the middle of a cloud the onboard TV camera with its infra-red equipment would provide the view of the outside world on a pop-up TV screen on the flight deck.

Wally left the lights of Liverpool behind and came to a hover over the Irish Sea. He gave Bert the order to atomise some of the sea water and create a Cumberland Grey cloud around them.

"How many gallons do you want boss?" enquired Bert.

"I think two million gallons will do. We don't want to overdo it."

"Ok boss!"

Within thirty minutes the Discovery was at the heart of a sizeable Cumberland Grey cloud, a type designed to keep folks guessing – will it or will it not rain? With the cloud created, the Discovery could move to the mouth of Morecambe Bay and hover there until it was time to move off and do the job tomorrow. Once in the hover, Wally and Bert could get their heads down for a good night's sleep. Everything was in place and ready to drizzle.

The holidaymakers on Morecambe beach were busy dedicating themselves to either sleeping, eating, sunbathing or castle-building. A small number ventured into the icy cold water to test their own virility whilst others embarked on a spree of ice cream licking or donkey riding or both but in the case of the latter it was a bit of a problem getting the licks on target. No-one was thinking of drizzle or desired it.

Around 1-00pm The Discovery started to move. A westerly wind of about two knots propelled the Cumberland Grey slowly toward its destination whilst the four silent running fan duct motors kept it at five thousand feet. No-one on the beach at Morecambe observed what was heading their way. Around 2-30pm the single incoming cloud was clearly visible. Its isolated position in the sky made it noticeable but still no-one paid it any attention.

At 2-45pm Abigail's voice boomed out across the sandy beach via the P.A. system loudspeakers.

"If you look out to sea you will see the cloud that will drizzle on you at 3-00pm."

"Load of old nonsense!" was typical of the many comments made by the sun seekers but they couldn't deny that there was a cloud approaching. Sleepers kept one eye open, sandwich eaters ate faster, but the castle-builders, bikini-clad sunbathers and bikini spotters took no notice at all;

at least they didn't until the shadow cast by the Discovery reached them. Suddenly the prominent puffy job in the sky had them all guessing and they all looked up in anticipation.

At 3-00pm on the dot, Wally gave the order to 'let em have the drizzle' and Bert complied, whilst down at ground level Abigail started her stop watch.

"Well I would never have believed it," said many of the holiday makers as they felt the first drizzle on their skin. The effect was amplified by the sun being masked by the cloud above them and it got steadily darker as Wally took the Discovery down from five thousand feet to one thousand. Initially there was much cheering and clapping to congratulate someone for making drizzle at the exact time they said they would, but no-one knew who, and it didn't last. Sleeping in drizzle is not the nicest of experiences and neither is sunbathing. Castle-builders got angry as their creations got diluted and fell apart. Bikini spotters lost interest and headed for the pubs, whilst the sandwich eaters gave up on soggy butties. All in all, there was an exodus from the exposed beach and sun seekers developed bad tempers as they had to relocate. By the time the drizzle had ceased, which was after fifty three minutes and twenty two seconds, the novelty had clearly worn off and the beach was empty.

Abigail had to contact the winner of the £100 prize and got a mouthful of abuse in the process. She contacted Wally and suggested that at the next venue it would be advisable to shorten the duration of future drizzles and this they did. Blackpool, Southport, New Brighton and Rhyl all got their drizzle although its popularity with the Local Authorities was somewhat diminished. The object of fundraising was a great success, with the generous British holiday makers making huge contributions, but it baffled those from overseas who could never understand the British attitude to weather.

Who is the prettiest?

Llandudno had agreed to host a Cloud Beauty Parade on its promenade to help raise funds. As well as paying a large sum to host the event, holidaymakers would be encouraged to make donations whilst observing the unique event. A panel of judges would decide which of the parading clouds was the prettiest and a suitable award would be made.

The idea for this had been the brainwave of Sunny Blue, the skipper of the Flier, who had spent a lifetime leering at costume clad female beauties at the many Bathing Beauty contests that are held each year around the country. But how on earth a cloud can be made to look pretty proved to be a challenge for all those operating out of Wythenshawe Weather Centre and restricted the number of contest applicants to six.

A set of rules was drawn up and, in simple terms, each cloud was to take the form of a Westmorland White and each was to be made up of no more than 2,000,000 gallons of atomised sea water. The six applicants would form up in a line facing Rhyl front before moving off at five minute intervals to Llandudno. On arrival, each cloud would face the audience on the promenade whilst the judges made notes, and then move on to make way for the next cloud to be judged. When all six had appeared before the judges they would all position themselves in a final line-up for one last viewing and then disperse. To make it more attractive it was agreed that the contest would be held in the evening as dusk was settling and the clouds could use their luminance equipment to make them glow. That should produce some excellent effects, thought the Council organisers.

All six applicants gave a great deal of thought as to how best they could make their clouds look and they had to use their own ideas for, as far as they knew, no cloud beauty parades had ever been held in the past. All six cloud machines were thoroughly checked over in Wythenshawe's huge hangar before they finally got airborne and headed to a water source to make a cloud. Each of the applicants had arranged to fly to separate locations where each would make adjustments to their good cloud looks. Each was anxious to look their best. At each of the six locations a ground observer in radio contact would issue advice until the final touches had been made.

"Cor, this is like having a cloud perm!" exclaimed Peter Arnolds, the Flight Engineer aboard the Softly Blows.

From Stranraer to Fleetwood, people in their thousands got a preview of one of the contest entries and most were entertained by what they saw, although in some cases they wondered what all the fuss was about. In due course, the six contenders made their way to Rhyl and lined up on the front prior to the big event.

It was a lovely evening in Llandudno and a huge crowd had gathered on the promenade to watch the Cloud Beauty Parade. No-one had ever heard of such a thing and hence there was a tremendous novelty value associated with it and nobody wanted to miss it. The crowds gathered sat in their thousands on both deck chairs and others that they had brought with them and looked earnestly at the sky which was beginning to darken. To keep everyone entertained, the Council had booked the famous Leyland Brass Band and they played splendid music most befitting to the occasion.

The music stopped and an announcement heralded the arrival of the first cloud.

"The first cloud beauty you will see this evening will be the Flier, crewed by her skipper, Sunny Blue, and if you look to your right you will observe its arrival."

All eyes craned to the right and a glowing Westmorland White cloud could be seen gracefully making its way towards Llandudno front. On arrival at a position opposite the judges, the Flier stopped and seemed to turn to face them but it is difficult to tell if a cloud is turning. In full glow the Flier looked splendid and drew many compliments from the audience who reckoned it had more curves than an army of females.

The Band struck up after a couple of minutes and the Flier moved on to make room for the next candidate. The PA system sprang to life again.

"The next cloud beauty to arrive from your right will be the Dismal, skippered by Snowy White."

The crowd had got into the spirit of things and started to clap as the Dismal made its slow way to face the judges. It may have been Dismal by name but it was more like its skipper's name than dismal. The snowy white glow was almost too much to look at and several pairs of sunglasses appeared amongst the audience. The secret of the Dismal's extra whiteness was down to some washing whitener that Snowy had put into the mixer on board the Dismal. Having been thoroughly looked at by the judges, the Dismal joined the Flier, making room in the process for the next cloud.

"Your next cloud beauty is the Spitting, skippered by Windy Blower, now making its way to the front of the panel of judges."

The crowd cheered and clapped again but announced a little disappointment since it was not that much different from the first two. It was glowing nicer than the first but not as good as the second. It had lots of curves but there was no telling if they were in the right place. No-one had ever established where a cloud's curves should be. Later, the Spitting was disqualified. Evidently, Windy had not used sea water, he had sought out the very best to make his cloud and that was against the rules.

"Look to your right and you will see the fourth of this evening's contenders."

Now this was different and oohs and aahs accompanied the clapping.

"This contender is the Softly Blows and her skipper is Lucy Windrush."

"I might have known it was a woman Skipper," announced a member of the audience as the pearly white Softly Blows with blue tints made its way majestically to face the panel of judges.

"Well that's different!" and "I wonder how she did that?" were typical of the comments being made about the Softly Blows.

It was beginning to cool off by now and flasks started to appear as members of the audience began to fortify themselves against the cold. But soon their attention was diverted to the next candidate.

"Coming from the right, the next cloud beauty is called the Skylark and its skipper is Bill Jones."

There was never going to be a problem remembering the Skylark; it was completely red. Just like a flaming red ball but in cloud form. It had the form of a Westmorland White but not its colour but it certainly added to the evening's spectacle and most were very impressed by it. The general opinion seemed to be that you couldn't beat it and it was a hot contender for first place in the contest.

In due course it was time for the final contender to grace the darkened evening sky and thousands of necks craned to see its arrival. They were not disappointed by what they witnessed.

"Our final contender this evening," the rest of the announcement was almost drowned out "is the Astro and is skippered by Albertino Insomnia."

The crowd were almost in hysterics as they saw a glowing, multi-coloured Mohican style cloud gliding into view before hovering in front of the judges. Photographs had been taken all evening but never as many as now for this was truly unique and there was much applause.

The Flier, Dismal, Spitting, Softly Blows, Skylark and Astro made a final parade in front of the appreciative audience, whilst Leyland Band provided suitable brass band music bringing the Cloud Beauty Parade to a conclusion. Only the judges' choice now remained and people left with mixed feelings after victory went to skipper Sunny Blue aboard the Flier.

But who cared, it had been a brilliant evening and so unusual and the crowd's appreciation was shown by the donations they made. The roof fund for 'The Head in the Sky' was climbing just like the cloud contenders now heading out to sea to rid themselves of their current manifestations. Cloud Beauty Contest or no, there was a limit and this exceeded it.

Who can glide the furthest?

Abigail came up with an interesting fundraising idea that would test the skills of any cloud machine skipper and the public could take a bet on the winner. She challenged skippers to atomise 4,000,000 gallons of water and create a Westmorland White cloud and proceed to Douglas on the Isle-of-Man. On arrival at Douglas the clouds were to hover whilst obtaining details of the prevailing wind. Armed with the wind details they were then to ascend to a height from which they could glide to Blackpool using the wind as their source of propulsion. Without any help from their fan duct motors each cloud would slowly descend, but if the skipper had done his sums correctly would reach its destination just as it was about to hit ground level. Whoever did this would be declared the winner.

Both in Blackpool and Douglas the bookies did a roaring trade and considerable amounts of money exchanged hands. The 'Cloud Glide' was being eagerly awaited. Six machines had been entered and these were the Nimbus, the Flier, the Hurricane, the Astro, the Skylark and the Drip. The Drip was piloted by Arthur Treadmill's brother Ronnie since Arthur was currently suspended. The favourite was the Hurricane, which was not surprising since its skipper was Abigail Windrush whose idea all this was. She was sure to have worked everything out in advance.

The six cloud machine crews had all gathered at Wythenshawe Weather Centre the day before the competition, and went through the usual rituals of checks and provisioning and then waiting for dark before getting their naked machines airborne. Once airborne they headed for the Irish Sea and each made a Westmorland White out of 4,000,000 gallons of sea water before flying to Douglas and hovering for the night at three thousand feet. The crews slept through to the following dawn and it was no hardship to the town of Douglas. Having cloud cover at night made no difference in the dark, but it was disappointing in the morning being hidden from the sun.

The organisers had arranged for the event to start at 9-00am and there would be an interval of one hour between each cloud departing. They had also determined the order in which the clouds would depart. The scene at Douglas was set for the big off. There were a surprising number of spectators about on the promenade. The usual newspaper purchasers were around along with those who had come to clear their lungs after a night of heavy smoking and those with a genuine interest in what was happening.

High above Douglas, in the six hidden cloud machines the crews were all busy making calculations. It was sixty nautical miles from Douglas to Blackpool and the wind was a north-westerly, blowing at fifteen knots which meant it would take four hours to glide that distance. Without their fan duct motors working each cloud would slowly descend, so the key to success was to start off at the right altitude. If they got that right they should land on Blackpool prom four hours after leaving Douglas.

Each of the six Westmorland Whites ascended to the altitude their calculation had determined and they confirmed to ground control that they were ready. The organisers looked at their watches and at precisely 9-00am they gave the signal to the Flier to start its glide. A canon was fired to announce the start to the general public but it was a bit of a shock to some, especially those still in bed.

The Flier started from an altitude of 5,000 feet and its skipper, Sunny Blue, was confident that this would win him the competition. The fan duct motors that were currently keeping the Flier in the hover were switched off and the wind propelled it forward on the journey to Blackpool. At 10-00am the Flier had descended to 3,500 feet with forty five nautical miles to go. Sunny was a little concerned at the rate of descent but for the moment did not intend to do anything about it. Abigail Windrush left Douglas at this time aboard the Hurricane but she did so from an altitude of 7,000 feet.

At 11-00am the Astro, skippered by Albertino Insomnia, departed Douglas from 4,000 feet. It was lucky he remembered to start. He was not the most reliable of individuals. Out in the Irish Sea the Flier was thirty nautical miles from Blackpool and down to 2,000 feet. Sunny was going to have to do something and soon.

Abigail was forty five nautical miles from Blackpool and down to 5,500 feet and was happy with the progress the Hurricane was making.

At noon it was time for the Skylark to depart and it left from a height of 6,000 feet. Its skipper, Bill Jones, was at the helm and was glad to be off. The Astro was forty-five nautical miles out from Douglas and down to 2,500 feet. The Hurricane was half way to Blackpool and down to 4,000 feet whilst the leading cloud, the Flier, was in a desperate state being down to 500 feet with fifteen nautical miles left to glide. Its skipper, Sunny Blue, decided to take the illegal step of atomising to increase the size of his cloud and improve its level of buoyancy. He was spotted by an observer on board one of the gas rigs in the Irish Sea and was immediately disqualified from the event.

The crowd on Blackpool front at 1-00pm were fully expecting the arrival of the first gliding cloud and were disappointed when the PA system erected for the event announced that the Flier had been disqualified for atomising and had subsequently dropped out of the competition. There would be no arrivals until 2-00pm. Over the Irish Sea, the Hurricane was only fifteen nautical miles away at 2,500 feet whilst the Astro was thirty nautical miles away and alarmingly, down to 500 feet. The Skylark was fifteen nautical miles out from Douglas and down to 4,500 feet and, back at Douglas, Cirrus Cumulus had just commenced his glide in the Nimbus starting at 6,000 feet. Cirrus was pleased that he had finally got underway.

By 2-00pm the crowd had re-gathered on Blackpool prom to witness the arrival of the Hurricane, and the PA system announced it. The Hurricane was spotted a good distance out and it seemed like an eternity before it finally reached them and when it did it soared 1,000 feet overhead, clearing the Tower easily. It was not going to hit land until it was well beyond Blackpool and that ruled Abigail out of the competition – the favourite had gone! Back out at sea, the Astro had hit it before having glided forty nautical miles, so that was another machine out of the contest. The Skylark seemed to be doing well, having glided to the halfway point and having descended to 3,000 feet. The Nimbus was also doing well, having reached the quarter way point at 4,500 feet. Back at Douglas the last cloud, the Drip, was just departing at an altitude of 6,000 feet. All these details were being relayed to the crowd at the finish point by the PA system. By this time many had concluded that the preferred starting height at Douglas was 6,000 feet and they noted that three of the competitors had started at this height.

There was a gap in arrivals at 3-00pm since the Astro had hit the sea, but the Skylark, Nimbus and Drip were all on their way. The Skylark was fifteen nautical miles out at 1500 feet and the Nimbus was thirty nautical miles out at 3,000 feet. Forty-five nautical miles out, the Drip was already experiencing difficulties and was now at 7,000 feet and its skipper, Ronnie Treadmill, couldn't fathom out what was happening.

By 4-00pm, amongst the crowd on Blackpool front there was keen anticipation that the first gliding cloud was about to land on them. The progress of the Skylark had been followed keenly by listening to the PA system but when 4-00pm arrived there was no Skylark in sight. People got fidgety and they started to demand information. A full ten minutes past before the organisers were able to inform everyone that the Skylark had landed at Lytham St.Annes. Bill Jones, the Skylark's skipper had drifted south as he made his journey across the Irish Sea. This was all turning out to be a bit of a damp squib as far as the public was concerned. But there were still two competitors left in it, the Nimbus with fifteen nautical miles to go and the Drip with thirty. The Nimbus at 1,500 feet seemed best placed for victory whilst the Drip was continuing its journey skyward being now at 8,000 feet.

As time started to approach 5-00pm, excitement was in the air. It seemed most likely that the Nimbus was going to succeed where others had failed and, with luck, it should embrace them all very shortly. The Nimbus headed steadily down towards its waiting crowd and before they were really prepared for it they were surrounded by a wet cloud that clung onto naked flesh and clothes alike and visibility dropped to almost nil along with the temperature. In the middle of this wet mist, the cloud machine that housed its skipper, Cirrus Cumulus and his Flight Engineer Puffy White, remained at its centre some one hundred feet or so above the ground and invisible to all. Cirrus made radio contact with the organisers to confirm his arrival just in case they hadn't noticed. With that done, the Nimbus lifted off taking its damp cargo of cloud with it leaving a very damp and irate group of individuals below them. But at least they got their sun back. The winner couldn't be announced until the arrival time of the last gliding cloud had been reached even though there was no-one left that could beat the Nimbus now. The Drip was only fifteen nautical miles out but at 9,000 feet it was out of the running or perhaps that should be gliding.

Ronnie Treadmill couldn't let things go on the way they were with the Drip and, after exhaustive checks, discovered that the fan duct motors had not been fully throttled back and the control column was slightly pulled toward him. This had given a slight angular displacement from the horizontal to the motors and that coupled with the low power setting was enough to make it ascend. The Drip passed over Blackpool Tower at 6-00pm at 10,000 feet ruling it well out of the competition and mostly well out of sight of those assembled on the front to witness the end of the event.

A few lucky individuals had made a bomb out of the bookies but the rest home at Grange-over-Sands had too and the residents were well on the way to having a new roof. A couple more events should do it!

Guess how many

The fourth fundraising event was staged at Llandudno. After the 'Prettiest Cloud Contest' the Local Authority felt it was worth exploring other cloud ideas and, after consultation with Wythenshawe Weather Centre, it was agreed to stage a 'Guess how many cloud machines were up there' competition. The details of this were carefully worked out and a plan made.

The competition involved the general public registering to participate and paying a fee which would go towards the roof replacement at 'The Head in the Sky' rest home. At precisely 3-00pm on a day when the weather was suitable, the public would have to guess how many of the clouds above them were not of nature's creation. Tucked in amongst the genuine puffy stuff would be an undisclosed number of volunteer cloud machines, and they would reveal themselves at ten minutes past the hour by switching on their luminance controls and glow amongst the natural masses. Punters would soon be able to tell if they had guessed correctly or not. The council would provide the prizes.

Surprisingly Mr Spite was inundated with volunteers to help with this event but in due course he picked those that he thought were most reliable. The volunteers assembled and checked their respective machines before getting together their provisions. Being weather-dependent there was no telling how long this event would last. With all the preliminaries out of the way the cloud machines got airborne at night and headed out to sea to create a cloud and then took up station several miles off the North Wales coast and hovered. They would remain here until the conditions were just right for the competition to be staged.

On the Llandudno promenade posters were pinned up daily to keep holidaymakers updated as to the weather conditions and the likelihood of the 'Guess How Many' competition being staged. Monday began with clear blue skies and it was decided that this would not be conducive to the staging of the event but there was considerable debate about it. The next two days it rained solidly from a sky full of grey stuff in every direction and the organising committee started to fall out about the wisdom of not going ahead on the Monday. To add to the committee's frustration, the volunteer crews were beginning to get bored. In the confined space of a cloud machine there was not a lot you could do when you were just hovering, and each day seemed longer than the last.

When Thursday arrived there was a sigh of relief. The sky was full of scattered clouds and it all looked ideal but it was still cold. It was a day when goose pimples started round your ankles and disappeared up your trouser leg before emerging again under your collar. The decision was taken to go ahead and do it today. Posters were pinned up to announce the decision and vehicles with loudspeakers on top went around the town announcing the details. By 3-00pm a considerable throng of holiday makers had gathered on the promenade, complete with goose pimples, and all eyes gazed out over the sea. The cloud machine volunteers had been informed earlier that today was the big day and after taking up positions amongst nature's migratory lumps of vapour they waited for their departure time to arrive.

To arrive over Llandudno promenade at 3-00pm from fifteen nautical miles out, propelled by a ten knots wind would take the cloud machines one and a half hours. At 1-30pm the volunteers from Wythenshawe joined the convoy heading for Llandudno and the waiting crowd.

There seemed to be an endless procession of clouds passing over the prom and after a while it got a bit mesmerising, but for those in with a chance of winning something there was to be no exit from the scene. The minutes ticked away and the clouds came and went. Many hoped that the intense study they were giving to the clouds would enable them to pick out any false bugger up there masquerading as the real thing. The countdown started at five to three and a silence fell as necks craned to cloud-spot. The never ending convoy continued flowing toward them, above them and beyond them but it was dead on 3-00pm that they had to make a decision and then the trouble started.

Once a person had decided how many cloud machines were up there, they had ten minutes to register their results before the cheats would identify themselves by glowing in the sky. The Local Authority had strategically placed a number of tents along the prom for punters to go to give in their guess but that proved woefully inadequate and by the time the Wythenshawe crews identified themselves by glowing, not everyone had filed their guess and people were being turned away. Chaos broke out and riots started. In panic, the nine cloud machines, which by now had left the scene on the prevailing wind, were asked to return and rain as heavily as possible.

Drenched punters left the scene in droves as the rain pelted down and the council workers in the tents beat a hasty retreat to the Town Hall which would be the focus for a protest when the rain finally stopped. The results of the competition were largely forgotten by now but that was not the cloud machine's problem, they had done the job they had volunteered for and it was time to go home.

Several days later, Mr Spite informed the 'Guess How Many' volunteers that a considerable amount of money had been raised as a result of their participation at Llandudno and the Local Authority had apologised for any embarrassment caused. Evidently, the success of the event had taken them by surprise but they had learned from the experience and would be more prepared next time. It was also the view of the Local Authority that Llandudno may be heading for a prestigious award for innovation and the title of Britain's cloud capital, but Blackpool might dispute that.

A final event

Prudence McWhirter sat down in her office and went over the amount of funds that had been raised for the essential replacement of the roof on the 'Head in the Sky' rest home. As Head of Care she felt a deep obligation in maintaining the standard of the building which would be the final home for a good proportion of its residents. Grant applications had raised £50,000. The Open Day, together with the many donations that were made as a result of it, raised another £50,000 which took her funds to half that which was needed. The volunteers from Wythenshawe Weather Centre had been magnificent and the combination of a 'Guess How Long the Drizzle Will Last', a 'Prettiest Cloud Contest, a 'Guess Who Can Glide the Best' and a 'Guess How Many of us There Are' Competition had gone on to take the total of funds raised to the grand sum of £195,000. Only five thousand pounds more was needed.

Prudence and Mr Spite C.D.M. from the Weather Centre in Wythenshawe got their heads together to generate a final fundraising scheme. Mr Spite was very keen to make the last event both a fundraising event and one of jubilant celebration. The only appropriate place for this to happen would be at Grange-over-Sands which would allow the home's current residents to pay homage to their wonderful host and carer, Prudence McWhirter. With a degree of reservation, Prudence agreed but being a rather reserved kind of person she really didn't want to face being in any kind of limelight; that was not her nature.

It was felt that a second Open Day was not a viable proposition but Mr Spite remembered the occasion when the world famous Leyland Brass Band had been shipped out to St.Kilda to give a thank you concert for the personnel stationed there, and he remembered what a stunning impact that had had both on the Islanders and the passengers aboard the cruise liner that had taken them there. The publicity had been phenomenal. Why not get Leyland Brass Band to conduct a concert in the grounds of the 'Head in the Sky' and why not get them to play some of Lucy Pankhurst's compositions that had gone down so well on St.Kilda? The grounds could accommodate 250 and chairs could be hired in. If the concert was by ticket only and it was properly advertised then there was a good chance that the last £5,000 could be raised. Mr Spite, casting his mind back to St.Kilda, had another idea up his sleeve but he was not going to let the cat out of the bag. It would be a special surprise for Miss McWhirter.

Advertisements went out in all the local newspapers and information spread around the whole of Cumbria regarding the evening concert being held in the grounds of the cloud machine crews' rest home at

Grange-over-Sands. Posters appeared on hoardings around the county and fliers were posted through many letter boxes. Local radio and TV did features highlighting the superb quality of Leyland Brass Band and its international standing as well as awarding accolades to the composer Lucy Pankhurst and her work that would feature in the concert. Great play was made of the concert held on a cruise liner in Village Bay on the remote island of St.Kilda and, most interestingly, reference was made to a very special activity that helped to make it all a most memorable and unique event the likes of which would be repeated at Grange-over-Sands. The latter point attracted the media who immediately paid large sums of money for the rights to cover it. The concert was a sell out well before it was due to take place and the fund target had already been reached due to the royalties coughed up by the media.

The grounds of 'The Head in the Sky' were quite a sight with some 250 people seated in front of the World famous Leyland Band, who were all smartly turned out in white jackets and dark trousers. Their brass instruments shone in the evening sun and waited to be played. The TV and Radio people had brought a considerable amount of equipment in order to ensure that they gave good coverage of the concert. The home's residents had pride of place and the Band's Musical Director paid them compliments before beginning. Eager anticipation could be detected in the audience and as soon as the Band began to play there was a realisation that this was not just any old band. The sound was magnificent and the choice of pieces played carefully matched the occasion. Two compositions by Lucy Pankhurst featured, 'The Great Cloud Parade' and 'St.Kilda's Fling', and before each piece was played Lucy was asked to explain to the audience the background to each one.

As the concert progressed the light faded and about half way through the second half, in the distant night sky a glowing Union Jack appeared to be heading towards the venue and it continued to do so until its arrival overhead. Its arrival coincided with the final piece of music and the appreciative audience stood and applauded; they had witnessed something that very few human beings ever get the chance to see and it was wonderfully received.

After the last number was played, Mr Spite invited Prudence McWhirter to join him. He gave a short introductory speech before handing over to

Prudence a cheque for £205,000. Prudence was overcome with emotion and for a time couldn't bring herself to speak but she summoned her reserve of character and thanked everybody on behalf of the residents, herself, and The Guild of Cloud-Owners' and finally, all those volunteers from Wythenshawe Weather Centre who not only raised a lot of money but also put the flag in the sky this evening. Her passionate thanks were well received and she left the limelight with her head held high and the band played on as she did so. Most important of all, a few days later, work began to replace the roof.

 # NEW EU RULES

Disturbing news

It was great to have nothing to do for a change and Cirrus and his faithful companion Puffy were both taking a well earned rest in their Slaidburn home. The sun was shining and the view from the lounge window was tranquil. The greenness of the countryside, the trees and meandering river induced a grand feeling of contentment. The grazing cattle added the finishing touches to the England that both of them loved so much. It is indeed scenes like this that made them wish and hope it would never change. Like so many other good folks there was a strong desire for a period free from change, a time for stability, for reassurance of their place in society. The feeling was enhanced by the fact that the crew of the Nimbus had been to a concert the previous day at Chorley Town Hall to listen to Leyland Brass Band who were fresh back from Oslo representing Great Britain in the European Brass Band Championship. The concert had been splendid. The music was at times most moving but it was also very British and just what the Nimbus crew liked.

The break from fundraising was particularly welcome; it had been a very busy time. Cirrus cast his eye on the latest framed certificate that graced the lounge wall. The certificate complimented the crew of the Nimbus for successfully gliding from Douglas in the Isle-of-Man to Blackpool and landing on the promenade at the end of it to raise lots of cash for 'The Guild of Cloud-Owners' rest home in Grange-over-Sands. The certificate made no mention of the fact that it had thoroughly soaked everyone that had turned out to welcome its arrival. Least said the better on that score but it was nice to have the accolade on show.

The Nimbus had also taken part in the 'Guess How Many Fake Clouds' you can see competition, although Cirrus disliked what he made being called fake. There was nothing unreal about the clouds he manufactured, they compared favourably with the best that nature could come up with. In fact, the Nimbus was able to improve on what nature produced or at least he thought so. It was a pity though that he and his colleagues had had to be called back to Llandudno to quell a riot with a heavy downpour at the end but that was not his responsibility.

The last fund raising event had definitely been the most complicated in terms of the involvement of cloud machines. The versatility of the machines produced in deeper Salford by Black, Black & Blackemore's certainly proved itself on the day the flypast took place over the 'Head in the Sky' rest home at Grange-over-Sands. The fitting of mixer machines aboard each cloud machine had been a great idea and allowed clouds of all sorts of colours to be produced. The effect of colouring had been further enhanced by the design and fitting of the luminance equipment which allowed skippers to make their clouds, coloured or otherwise, to glow. It had to be agreed that the effect was best seen using coloured clouds.

To create a glowing Union Jack flag in the sky was no easy task. First a plan was made which allocated a position and colour to each of the many cloud machines taking part and each one was allocated a number. The illuminated flag had to be rehearsed and this had been done over Morecambe Bay. An observer in a boat had anchored in the bay to observe the clouds above. To begin with they had their luminance equipment switched off. Using a radio, the observer called up each cloud machine in number order and gave instructions for each to switch its luminance equipment on and to move to a position that matched his Union Jack flag cloud layout plan. When each cloud was in its correct position and the flag was to his satisfaction he temporarily handed over to the lead cloud machine who then fixed his height with his altimeter, having set its pressure with the aid of a radio call to Blackpool airport. The leader then called all his colleagues to set their altimeters in the same way and then to ascend or descend as the case may be to the same altitude as himself. When all the clouds were at the same height the Union Jack looked sharp and focussed. The final part of rehearsing was to fly in formation and keep in formation so that the Union Jack flag continued to fly appropriately in the sky. Having had previous experience of flying the flag, the challenge on this occasion was not too difficult.

A regular ferry service for commercial vehicles operates daily from Heysham on the east coast of Morecambe Bay to Carlingford in Northern Ireland, but not usually with giant size Union Jack flags forming in the skies above them as they depart or arrive. There is no record of the comments made by the people on board any of these vessels but rumour has it that the language was equally as coloured as the clouds in the sky, but mostly blue.

The Union Jack, when perfected and able to travel without unravelling, had to hover until a signal was received to start 'flying the flag'. Time was critical, as was the course they must fly, but the leader had been fully briefed. At the correct height and speed the Union Jack flag passed over several landmarks to arrive overhead 'The Head in the Sky' rest home at exactly the appointed time to coincide with the final piece of music being played by Leyland Band. The crews on board the participating clouds could see the audience below standing and applauding. They couldn't hear the music but that was of no consequence, they had done what was asked of them and they all got the chance to see the reports on TV and hear about it on the radio, not to mention reading about it in the newspapers.

Thinking back on what they had been involved in, Cirrus and Puffy could be well pleased with themselves. It had been a great experience and most importantly, the rest home would be getting a new roof.

Thoughts now turned to other things. For some time Cirrus had been thinking about giving his home a name but think as he did he couldn't come up with anything suitable. He took inspiration from the many things he had done with the Nimbus and drew up a list:

1. Cloud Parade
2. Lake Filler
3. Cloud Help
4. Aurora Cloudealis
5. St.Kilda's Fling
6. Guiding Cloud
7. Fund Raiser

8. Great Drizzler
9. The Nimbus
10. Cloud Drifter

"Puffy, take a look at this list will you?"

"What's this all about skipper?" asked Puffy.

"I want to give the house a suitable name and these are ideas that I have come up with. What do you think?"

"That's easy," said Puffy. "I would call it Aurora Cloudealis, it sounds really posh!"

And so it came to be. The home of the Nimbus crew was called the Aurora Cloudealis and the name appeared on the front gate as well as on a nicely painted name board that was fixed on the front of the house to one side of the front door.

Aurora Cloudealis was a name that created a fair bit of interest amongst the inhabitants of Slaidburn village but they had become relatively accustomed by now to the comings and goings of the crew of the Nimbus who invariably had stories to tell after a couple of pints in the Hark-to-Bounty pub, and they always sounded a bit far-fetched.

Girls, girls, girls

Spending so much time with their heads in the cloud, so to speak, it shouldn't be so surprising that thoughts should turn to the subject of girls. Neither Cirrus nor Puffy could be described as being in the prime of their life but they had nevertheless established amorous relationships with two glamorous ladies who were somewhat younger than themselves. Both females were in the same line of business as the crew of the Nimbus and as a result, weather-making and delivering kept them apart for considerable periods of time.

Abigail Windrush was skipper of the Hurricane and Cirrus could not get over the fact that she had taken a strong liking to him. Being rather reserved and a bit shy when it came to all things female, Cirrus could not have been chosen by anyone as the perfect match for Abigail but he was most happy with the situation. Being as he was, he felt awkward as well as happy and this was observable when they met, but it was also one of those things that attracted Abigail to him.

On the other hand, Puffy was a more gregarious character and never short in coming forward when it came to members of the opposite sex. His appetite for women was currently being kept under strict control by Carol Aspinall who was the Flight Engineer aboard the Astro. To say that Carol was a bit of an extrovert would not be over exaggerating. When not on cloud duty she would dress in a style that suited her personality and Puffy loved her for it. The relationship between the two of them was borne out of a mutual acceptance of their differences along with a desire to test each other's wrestling skills.

"Captain!"

Cirrus always knew that when Puffy addressed him in this fashion he was about to ask for something and waited to find out what it was.

"We haven't seen the girls recently. Don't you think we should invite them over for a few days?"

"I think that's a splendid idea. You're right, we haven't seen them for some time but they may have a job on."

"There's only one way to find out skipper.

The first thing Abigail noticed as she arrived at the Slaidburn home of Cirrus a couple of days after being given the invite was its new name.

"I like your new house name Cirrus, it reminds me of that wonderful job we did at Portrush last year."

"I'm glad you like it. It took some time to think of a suitable name but I'm glad Puffy and I chose Aurora Borealis, it sounds special!"

"I wonder if the Riley Academy will promote the event again this year," pondered Abigail.

"I thought it was going to become an annual event", replied Cirrus.

The next thing to draw Abigail's attention was the new certificate on the lounge wall. She looked at it and studied it for a few moments but declined from saying anything. Abigail had been expecting to win the cloud gliding competition from Douglas in the Isle-of-Man to Blackpool and felt a little rankled at being beaten by Cirrus. If she made any comments about it she felt sure that her floating over Blackpool Tower and continuing the glide that would lead her to make a landing well east of the town would only bring laughs at her expense. Prudence was exercised and she cast her eyes elsewhere.

"Cirrus you never talk about your family."

"There isn't much to tell. My mother and father are both dead and I don't have a brother or sister."

"Where did your mother and father come from?"

"My father came from Leigh in Lancashire and my mother came from a place called Blaenavon in South Wales."

"How did they meet?"

"They met during the mid fifties. They both served in the Air Force and were stationed at a place called Bassingbourn. They married in 1962 and then in 1973 dad got posted to Hong Kong. My mother brought me up for the first two years of my life until dad came back home in 1975."

"Where did they settle?" asked Abigail.

"Dad got demobbed in 1976 and brought me and mum up to Lancashire to live. He got a job at Black, Black & Blackemore's in deeper Salford and when I got a bit older my mother worked in a Woolworths store in Leigh which is where we lived."

"So that's how you got to know about cloud machines," remarked Abigail.

"Yes, that's right and what about you, what about your family?"

"My mother and father are both dead as well. I have one sister, Lucy, who you already know."

"And where did your family come from Abigail?"

"My family came from Clitheroe. My mother and father both worked at the aircraft factory at Samlesbury and hey presto, here I am!"

"I suppose you learned about cloud machines through your parent's involvement at Samlesbury?"

"No I didn't. My sister Lucy and I joined the Air Cadets in Clitheroe and that's where we first heard about cloud machines."

Whilst Abigail and Cirrus were passing the time talking, Puffy and Carol engaged in their favourite pastime, namely, wrestling. They did not intend wasting any time, when all said and done, they did not see much of each other as it was so why not capitalise and see as much of each other now. The settee springs matched their love locks with corresponding squeals which interspersed their oohs and aahs.

More serious matters

After a couple of blissful days the girls had to leave: work called. Parting was getting more difficult especially for Cirrus, and Abigail was fully aware of it. Cirrus didn't think he could feel this way about anyone and didn't know how to cope with it but for the moment cope with it he must. In the case of Puffy and Carol, well, they needed time to breathe again after all the physical exertion they had shared and parting was less of a heartache.

With the departure of the girls there was nothing for it but to read the Daily Gloom, thought Cirrus. He wanted to find out what had been going on in the world whilst his back had been turned, but more than likely all he would achieve is the topping up of his depression. No matter how many times Puffy would encourage Cirrus to do something else he would still read the paper and end up depressed about something. The only saving grace was that the periods of depression were short-lived and Cirrus would rapidly bounce back to good form.

Reading the paper, the issues that interested Cirrus were pretty much the same as before. Nothing seemed to change. No issues had been resolved. Immigration from both inside and outside the European Union seemed to be contributing to a range of problems but most important of them in the mind of Cirrus was the way it was changing the nature of the country he knew and loved.

Now the focus turned to Foreign Aid and how the country could afford to give other countries money when it had to borrow money to do it. It just didn't add up or make sense; he couldn't conduct his own affairs in that way.

To add to the giving of money to other country's, Cirrus couldn't understand the wisdom of paying out pensions to people who have retired and gone to live abroad. Is that not another form of Foreign Aid? The pensions taken from the United Kingdom economy are destined to go into another country's economy. Can the UK afford that?

Cirrus was in full flow as he continued to read the bits of the paper that interested him and began to cast his mind to the subject of prisons. He posed the question of the wisdom of spending vast sums of money providing for murderers in prison. Can the country afford such humanitarian welfare for people who have shown no humanity to their victims? Why can prisons not be more basic than they are? What is the wisdom of spending huge amounts of money on prisoners whilst at the same time the country cannot afford to fund young people to go to University? Priorities seemed to be worked out by the political class in a way that Cirrus could not align himself with.

Puffy partially opened the door to the lounge and peered in to get some idea as to the mood of his captain. It was instantly clear by the way that Cirrus had his head buried in the paper that this would not be the best time to disturb him. He was clearly updating himself on the issues he thought mattered. If Puffy chose his time correctly and waltzed into the lounge with coffee and cake, the temper of his skipper's mood would have subsided, but this was easier said than done and he quietly closed the door and went about his jobs.

Now there's another thing, thought Cirrus. All these devolved governments that we have. The Welsh assembly, the Scottish assembly and the Northern Ireland assembly as well as the British Government, not to mention our MEPs, why do we need all these pen pushers in a country as small as ours? Can we really afford to pay all these people who make nothing, grow nothing, repair nothing and so on? It really is a form of madness, he thought.

Cirrus put the paper down for a moment as he tried to digest something he had just read, and his thoughts turned to what he thought was the most pressing issue of the times, the balance of payments. In his mind there was nothing simpler in life than the fact that you can't spend what you don't earn and if you do then you have to borrow money from someone and not only pay it back but pay them something for loaning it to you in the first place. This puts an extra strain on your already beleaguered funds and gets you in a permanent deficit trap that you can't get out of unless you perform serious surgery to cut your own spending. The United Kingdom had had to borrow money to buy the things it needed to fight and survive the Second World War and that generated huge debts. But that was a long time ago and there had, in the mind of Cirrus, been plenty time to pay that off. Cirrus hated the idea of paying anyone interest, it was money for money. It wasn't as if you were getting a car or a washing machine or having a job done; you were just giving someone money for money they had loaned you.

A full head of steam was developing as Cirrus moved from one page of the paper to another and when he arrived at an article on the European Union he almost blew a gasket. Those unelected European Ministers making laws by which we must live was just too much. Cirrus mused on the vast sums of money the United Kingdom pays into the European Union each year and how much of it comes back. There is a big deficit there, he thought. He mused on the advantages of being in a free trade agreement. The United Kingdom buys a lot more from the European Union than the other countries in the same Union buy from the United Kingdom. We suffer both a funding and a trade deficit. And what about the cost of all our Members of the European Parliament, do we need them?

That was enough depressing reading for one day thought Cirrus and he put the paper down but it would take some time to wind down. A few minutes passed and then a knock on the door announced Puffy's arrival.

"That's just what I needed Puffy, coffee and cake."

Blimey, thought Puffy, I really did think I was going to get it this morning.

"You know, I think I have the solution to this Country's burning problems!"

I thought too soon, thought Puffy.

"All these newspaper blokes have the answers. They tell you every day. I think they should get together and form a Press Party."

"You mean a Press Gang skipper."

"I like that Puffy, yes a Press Gang. They would be better than all these politician wallas!"

Talking about the EU

The latest edition of the Guild of Cloud-Owners' monthly journal, The Monthly Downpour, arrived at the Slaidburn home of the crew of the Nimbus and Puffy delivered it to his captain.

"You might find something interesting in this," said Puffy.

"What have you seen then? Is it another course that you think we should apply for?"

"Nothing like that skipper," said Puffy and he beat a hasty retreat before the conversation got any further.

Cirrus began to read this latest edition and it wasn't too long before he reached the page which had a heading that caught his eye – **New EU regulations being considered for cloud machines.** His first reaction was not complimentary.

"Damned EU! Who the devil do they think they are? There are no cloud machine operators in Europe other than those in Wythenshawe Weather Centre so what's it got to do with the EU?"

Puffy could hear his captain ranting from the other side of the house and instinctively knew that it would not be wise to share his space for the time being.

Cirrus read on and his indignation rose as he digested the ideas that the European Union were seriously considering with a view to making regulations to govern them. The article had been written by the Superintendant at Wythenshawe Weather Centre – Mr I.N.Spite C.D.M, who was urging all cloud machine owners to seriously read the proposals and then get back to him. He emphasised how important this was by outlining some of the possible implications for their weather business.

The ideas listed by Mr Spite seemed outrageous to Cirrus. **No raining on Sundays!** That was sheer lunacy he thought and he paused for several minutes before moving on to the next item. **A limit of 2,000,000 gallons to be imposed on any atomisation process!** That was a half of what they could do now, what on earth are they up to he thought before moving on again. **Tachograph to be fitted to all cloud machines!** What on earth do they want to do that for? **Imposing a speed limit!** This really is going too far, thought Cirrus.

"Puffy, Puffy!" shouted Cirrus.

Hearing his captain's call, Puffy made his way to the lounge with a degree of trepidation. He could tell from his skipper's tone that he was not very happy about something.

"Just look at all this," said Cirrus who went on, "This damned EU is driving me mad. Just take a look at what they are considering doing to us."

Puffy took the journal from his skipper and began to look at the article by Mr Spite. His jaw dropped and his mouth partially opened as he read the contents.

"No raining on Sundays, a limit of 2,000,000 gallons to be imposed on any atomisation process, a tachograph to be fitted to all cloud machines and imposing a speed limit! Well I wouldn't believe it skipper!"

"Well believe it or not, unless we protest it will happen and that's not all of it. I couldn't bring myself round to reading all the proposals. Just pass the journal back whilst I have another look."

The Captain read on and then jumped out of his chair in a rage.

"Just look at that!"

Puffy just looked at Cirrus in bewilderment for he couldn't read the journal being waved across his face and before he could speak Cirrus ranted on again.

"Now they want to impose **parking fees** on us."

"But we don't park."

"They mean hovering fees and not only that, they want to **ban flying in the opposite direction to nature's clouds whilst visible.** This is the absolute limit. We should get out of the EU before they ruin us."

"Aye, aye skipper," was all that Puffy could contribute.

Composing himself, Cirrus sat down again and read on whilst Puffy stood and prepared himself for the next outburst. He didn't have long to wait.

"Good God, I can't believe it, the EU want to **confine thunder and lightning to rural areas!** I'd like to thunder and lighten on Brussels after reading this lot."

Puffy simply hoped that this was the last item but it wasn't.

"And look at this for a mad idea, **refilling or topping up of lakes or reservoirs must be done with matching water,** they call it a like for like policy. Can you beat that?"

Of all the items that Cirrus had gone on about the latter was one that had some merit, thought Puffy, but wisely refrained from breaking the tempo of his captain's current onslaught.

Cirrus was not really sounding out the opinion of Puffy. He was simply using him as a sound board and when he was done with him he decided to give his colleague, Wally Lenticular, a telephone call.

"Hello Wally, its Cirrus here."

"Hello Cirrus, what can I do for you?"

"Have you seen the article by Mr Spite in the Monthly Downpour?"

"Which one, he submits quite a few?"

"The one about the things that the European Union are considering making regulations about!"

"Oh, that one! Yes I have and it's bloody scary. If they get their way it will spell an end to our work. Weather on demand will become weather of the past."

"That's just the way I feel about it too. I think we all need to get back to the superintendant and let him know our views."

In due course every single member of the Guild of Cloud-Owners' got back to Mr Spite and aired their views about the EU proposals to him and none were complimentary. Clearly an organised response was needed, but first it was important to establish why the various items being considered were not going to work and that would mean the organising of a debate. Mr Spite's secretary, Goldilocks, was going to be very busy.

The big debate

The large conference hall in Wythenshawe Weather Centre was teeming with cloud- owners on the day of the big debate. The whole idea of the EU imposing any kind of regulations on the weather workers had raised considerable animosity. Many owners were all too aware of the way in which the fishing industry in the UK had been decimated by EU regulations and they were determined that they would not be having any of it.

When Cirrus and Puffy walked into the hall they immediately recognised many colleagues and there was a lot of handshaking and fast small talk to establish what they thought, but that didn't take long. It was pretty obvious from the start that any attempt to regulate by the EU would be met by hostility.

When the Superintendant, Mr Spite C.D.M., entered the hall it was a signal for everyone to break off their conversation and to take their seats.

"Albertino, where are you taking that seat?" asked Mr Spite.

"Sorry Mr Spite, I thought you said take your seat!"

Mr Spite cut Albertino short and asked him kindly to sit down. The rest of the gathering laughed out loud and suddenly the hall was tension free.

"Typical Albertino!" remarked several of his colleagues.

Now it was time to get down to the serious stuff and those present looked at the prepared agendas that had been handed to them as they entered the hall. Mr Spite began, "Ladies, gentlemen, cloud-owners, cloud crew members, may I thank you all for taking the time to come to this serious debate."

"Get on with it will you!" shouted someone hidden at the back of the hall.

Mr Spite cleared his throat before continuing.

"You are now aware that the European Union is proposing to regulate our activities and you know the things that they are looking at. I propose that we look at each item in turn and come up with constructive reasons why it would be a bad idea."

"What happens if the EU doesn't agree with us?" asked someone.

"We can cross that storm when we come to it," replied Mr Spite.

The debate began by considering the first item on the agenda, namely, **no raining on Sundays.** Mr Spite outlined the reasoning behind the proposal.

"The EU feels that it would be beneficial to minimise raining as much as possible and since the only rain they may have any influence over is our rain, they have proposed that we don't do it on a Sunday. They also think that this would benefit the tourist trade, especially those resorts by the sea."

"And what countries proposed that idea?" asked one of the gathering.

"It was proposed by France, Italy and Spain."

"Typical isn't it? France, Italy and Spain are all happy to promote the well-being of their tourist industry but not our weather-making industry," shouted a vociferous member of the audience.

Mr Spite continued once more. "The EU also suggests that sports would also benefit from a day off from our raining, especially cricket and tennis, and there you have it gentlemen. It would benefit the tourist industry and sport. Now you have to respond."

Wally Lenticular was the first to stand and he replied, "We don't rain much on Sundays as it is and you can't stop nature raining. This is a daft idea."

The audience clapped and nodded in agreement.

Ben Jones was the second person to stand. "Droughts don't go away on Sundays and neither do forest fires or any other kind of fires and that's what we are good at taking care of."

Ben's comments received unanimous agreement; he had provided a very strong counter argument. Next up was Lucy Windrush and once the wolf whistles had died down she began, "There are some activities that positively need our rain on Sundays and the Chelsea Flower Show is an example."

This suggestion by Lucy also met with the approval of the audience and Mr Spite intervened at this point, telling everyone that a strong case had been made against this proposal and they should move onto the next item.

"The next proposal is to **limit the amount of water we can atomise at any one time to 2,000,000 gallons.** It is being proposed in order to preserve the scarce supply of certain grades of water. In addition, the EU is concerned at the speed at which water levels can fall when mass atomising takes place. This has led to many boats becoming beached at no fault of their owners."

Henry Black was the first to respond to this idea.

"This is a proposal that could be the death knell of our industry. If we are limited to atomising 2,000,000 gallons, which is half of our cloud machine capacity then it will take twice as long to complete each job and make it twice as expensive. It will be the end for us."

As Henry sat down there was a loud shout from the audience of "Hear, hear!" and then it was the turn of Sunny Blue.

"If this proposal goes through then there will be all kinds of things we will not be able to do properly. We could only do heavy rain for twenty minutes, a downpour for fifteen, a heavy downpour for ten. If we were requested to perform a monsoon it would only last five minutes. We could be prosecuted under the trade descriptions act."

Another round of "Hear, hear!" was followed by chants of agreement but before another speaker could address everyone Mr Spite interjected.

"Gentlemen, gentlemen, it's all very well pointing out the impact of such a proposal on our activities but what we need are valid counter arguments."

For a moment or two silence descended on the hall and it was some relief when Snowy White rose to address the gathering. "You are all forgetting a very important job that we are often called upon to do." Snowy paused and his audience waited expectantly for him to continue.

Snowy spoke one word, "Floods!"

"God, he's right, floods!"

"Floods don't go away without our assistance and it would not help if the amount of water we can take away from a location is halved. It's no good taking the water level down from the top of your bedroom window to the top of your living room window, you need to take it down to the ground level."

A huge round of clapping acknowledged that a good counter argument had been found and it was time to move on to the next item on the agenda.

"Item three on the agenda is the EU proposal to make it mandatory for **every cloud machine to have a tachograph installed**."

Before the Superintendant got much further, an uncomfortable amount of barracking threatened to bring proceedings to a halt, but Josh Harrop came to the rescue by commanding silence in his unique style by bawling out the words, "Belt up all of you!"

Mr Spite thanked Josh and began again. "The EU is arguing that all they are doing is bringing cloud machines into line with road haulage regulations. They also point out that by using a tachograph they can ensure that cloud crews do not work for longer hours than it is safe to do. They argue that tiredness leads to accidents and the tachograph would allow them to comply with health and safety regulations."

A number of members of the audience stood up at the same time to protest and Mr Spite had to point to one at a time to speak. Abigail Windrush was the first. "Can I point out that unlike road hauliers we don't carry goods. You can't classify the clouds we carry in the same way as a tin of beans."

She could not have chosen as bad a thing as a tin of beans for comparison for she left the floor open to the humour of her colleagues.

"We do have something in common with beans though – wind."

Next to speak was Peter Arnolds who pointed out that although the crew of a cloud machine may be on board for long periods of time they were not working for all that time. There were always opportunities to sleep. This point was reinforced by Abigail who described the many hours on a typical task when there was no work to be done at all, just waiting.

The speakers were coming thick and fast and Albertino Insomnia took the floor next to remind his colleagues that on a long flight it was usual to have a rota so that each crew member took it in turns to monitor the progress of their cloud. But just as he finished someone shouted out that Albertino usually slept through his periods of watch keeping and that helped to take a little of the emotion out of the debate. Carol Aspinall spoke next to highlight the fact that some crews tended to take an extra crew member on particularly long jobs and she was immediately offered at least half a dozen there and then.

Things got back onto a serious plane when Bert Drummond took the floor.

"I think we should point out that there is almost no evidence to indicate that any accidents involving cloud machines have been attributed to crew tiredness. We can from that point of view, not be compared with road hauliers and furthermore our highway in the sky is wider than all the motorways put side by side. The chances of bumping into each other are almost nil."

This was the kind of thing that Mr Spite wanted to hear; this was the kind of fact that the EU had to take note of.

"I'm going to move on now to item four on the agenda and then I think we should take a break. Item four relates to the proposal **to make it illegal to fly a cloud machine in the opposite direction to natural clouds whilst in view of the general public."**

General mayhem broke out and it didn't look as if it would come to a stop but once more Josh Harrop stepped in to save the day or at least the debate.

"Belt up you lot and I won't tell you again! There's enough hot air in here so save it and listen to what the Super has to say."

Strangely, Josh got a round of applause and Mr Spite thanked him once again.

"The view of the EU is that when some clouds are observed flying in the opposite direction to others or indeed across the path of others, it has an unnerving effect on some members of the general public which could lead to permanent mental damage. They are arguing the case on medical grounds."

Ben Jones was the first to speak on this matter.

"I think it should be made known that, generally speaking, when we have to fly in a different direction than nature's lot we either do it at night when it's dark or above the clouds when the sky is covered with a layer of stratus."

Mr Spite pointed next to Larry Oliver who stressed that on many jobs, especially when doing convoy work for Eddie Stormbart, a great deal of the time was spent flying over oceans or deserts and you don't tend to find many folks in these places to which there was general agreement.

Mr Spite stepped into the proceeding to stress that what had been said on the subject so far didn't amount to a strong argument to put to the EU.

After a prominent pause, Puffy White got up to speak much to the surprise of Cirrus and he went on, "I hope you haven't forgotten that natural clouds sometimes do the same as us. Yes they do! The currents of air high up in the sky can blow in very different directions than those down below and so you see, nature does make some clouds fly in opposite directions to others over a given point on the surface of the Earth and the EU can huff and puff as much as it likes but it won't stop that."

Members of the audience looked at each other as much in wonder at the quality of the way Puffy had made his case as well as the quality of the case he had put. He got a rousing response and as it died down his captain, Cirrus Cumulus, stood up for he did not want to be outdone by his Flight Engineer.

"As has been said in response to previous items on the agenda, there are circumstances in which worries about unnerving members of the general public must be overridden by other more pressing needs such as emergencies like floods, fires and severe droughts. Cloud machines, like any emergency vehicles, cannot be governed by restrictive practices that stop them carrying out their function."

Cirrus had made his case eloquently and Mr Spite was well pleased with the way things had gone so far.

"Ladies and gentlemen, I think it is time for us to take a well earned break. We will reconvene the debate in one hour's time."

More debating

After the break the cloud crews began returning and some looked slightly worse for wear. The Silver Lining Club had evidently done good business. As Mr Spite strode on to the stage, silence fell once more and he was able to get straight back into the business. He drew everybody's attention to item five on the agenda.

"Item five, as you can all see, refers to the intention of imposing **a speed limit on all cloud machines** but it does not say what that limit may be. The EU has concluded that there are a number of good reasons for doing this. First, they think it may minimise the risk of accidents and that it will bring cloud machines into line with the speed limitations imposed on road hauliers. Secondly, they think it will minimise any risk to gliders and hot air balloons. Thirdly and finally, they think it will help to prevent overtaking and racing. So there you are gentlemen, something else for you to chew over."

There was no shortage of individuals wanting to have their four-pennyworth and Mr Spite pointed to Jim Waters.

"There has never been a cloud accident that was caused by speeding so tell em to put that in their pipe and smoke it!"

Once the laughter had died down it was the turn of Nick Gerrard.

"Doesn't the EU know that we already have a speed limit imposed on us by the UK Government? It's all laid down in The Cloud Machine Operators Rules of Operation Manual?"

"That's a very good point Nick. Ok Peter, go ahead."

"I just want to say that we are not road transport. We don't drive on a highway. They can't compare us with road transport and what's more, road transport has a much higher speed limit than we do even with restrictions."

"Hear, hear!" shouted several members of the audience and Peter went on, "I would also like to say that the rules already applying to gliders and hot air balloons prohibit them from entering clouds."

After a further round of applause the final speaker on the subject said his piece.

"I think we come back to the same point we made to several other proposals and that is that if we have to deal with a flood or a fire or a drought or for that matter fighting crime, and I draw your attention here to the cricket fixing we were called upon to deal with recently, we cannot observe some bureaucratic speed limit."

This response from Lucy Windrush was met with unanimous approval.

"Let me move on now to item six, **parking fees**."

The debate temporarily descended into chaos and several minutes passed before the audience realised that there was not going to be any further debating until they all shut up. Josh Harrop couldn't come to the rescue this time for he was sound asleep at the back of the hall, having consumed several drinks in the Silver Lining Club during the break. Silence did however re-establish itself and Mr Spite continued.

"The EU in its infinite wisdom thinks that it is unfair to cast a shadow in one spot for prolonged periods of time. They say it cuts out the light and it cuts out the sun's heat. They also point out that it affects sporting events and cricket in particular."

The audience roared with laughter as several members told them to tell the EU what our weather was like normally.

A case against the proposal was called for and there was, as anyone might expect, a huge response but the main points listed were as follows:

1. Real clouds park or hover over one place regularly.
2. Cloud machines do most of their parking or hovering either at night or over the sea or sparsely populated areas.
3. Real clouds reduce heat and light. Is the EU going to charge nature and if so, where will the bill go?
4. Cloud machines deliberately go out of their way to avoid parking over sporting events and in the case of the recent cricket-fixing job, that had been an exception in order to capture criminals.
5. It is sometimes essential to park or hover over a given spot to put out a fire or quell a riot.

"Gentlemen I think we have established enough reasons to quash the proposals we have so far heard about, but there are still two more to deal with."

The debate was becoming a bit drawn out and some of its members were beginning to suffer the after-effects of taking a break in the Silver Lining Club. Josh Harrop was not alone!

"Item seven on the agenda deals with the proposal that **all water taken from a reservoir or lake must be replaced with water of the same quality.** The EU insists that people want to feel safe that they know what water they are drinking or what water they are swimming in or sailing on."

In principle this sounded all well and good but as the first respondent pointed out, water replacement was nature's business and that should be the end of it. But as is the case with human beings, and cloud machine crews in particular, that was not the end of it.

"I think we should let the EU know that whenever we do top up a lake or a reservoir we do try and use same for same water when requested, and an example of that was when Cirrus Cumulus and his machine the Nimbus refilled Lake Windermere."

Although the point was interesting it didn't add strength to the counter argument but the next comment was well received.

"Mr Spite, you know without me telling you, we do not take our cloud machines and rain to places where we are not wanted."

"Thank you for that," said Mr Spite.

It was a great relief to everybody when they reached the final item on the agenda, item eight. But it had to be delayed for a few minutes to accommodate something of a mass relief, first.

"The last item on the agenda is **Thunder and Lightning**. It is being proposed that cloud machines confine their thunder and lightning to rural areas only. Their general thinking is that cities and towns get enough without adding to it. They also think that it can damage people's health. Finally, the EU thinks that thunder and lightning should under no circumstances be used as a source of entertainment or pleasure."

At this point Mr Spite had to duck to avoid a meat pie heading in his direction. It missed, but collided with the wall behind where it impacted with such high velocity that it remained adhered to its surface before slowly sliding down to the floor, leaving a gravy trail behind it. Josh Harrop's awakening coincided with this event and he sprung to his feet shouting, "Who pinched my meat pie?" Laughter always follows events of this nature and this debate was no exception. On a more serious vein there were a number of speakers who between them highlighted the fact that only grade one class cloud machines had the ability to produce thunder and lightning and they were rarely called upon to provide it. Another speaker brought it to everyone's attention that animals were also frightened by thunder and lightning, so was it really fair restricting it to rural areas.

A great deal of discussion accompanied the topic of using thunder and lightning as a source of entertainment but the consensus was that wherever cloud machines had been asked to create a spectacle using this kind of weather it had always been received extremely well.

The debate was brought to a close by Mr Spite summarising the counter arguments to the EU's proposals and he went on to say, before wishing everyone a safe journey home, "If the worst comes to the worst and these proposals become European Law, we can consider moving our headquarters from Wythenshawe Weather Centre to a disused oil platform in the Irish Sea outside European territorial waters. That way we can work with impunity." Although this was well received generally, it did cause anguish in some quarters and that included Goldilocks, Mr Spite's secretary.

A SKY WITHOUT CLOUDS

An intriguing advert

Everything seemed to start with Cirrus Cumulus sitting in his lounge reading either the Daily Gloom or the journal of The Guild of Cloud-Owners', which was called the Monthly Downpour, and today was no different. There was a waft of bacon coming from the kitchen and Cirrus felt most comfortable in the knowledge that his morning treat was being prepared by his faithful engineer, Puffy White, and he turned his attention to his newspaper. Having read his stars, as was his usual starting place, he moved on in search of what would interest him. Having read the important stuff, he gave the paper one more scan for anything he may have previously missed and he spotted an advertisement that he thought was intriguing and he read on.

> **Fancy a sky without clouds and a guarantee it will happen?**
> **Why not try Vannin's Cloud Removers?**
> **Phone Vannin's with your blue sky requirements**

Cirrus thought he recognised the phone number and when Puffy entered the room with his morning coffee he showed him the advert and the phone number.

"That's the bloke who owned The Peel Wine and Spirits Company on the Isle-of-Man. You remember him; he wanted to make a Manx whisky with water that was half Manx and half Scottish."

"I remember him alright. I wonder what he's trying this time. I'm going to read a bit more."

As Cirrus read the text that accompanied the headline it became clear that this chap Vannin was claiming that he could get rid of clouds to order. Now that was interesting, he thought. How on earth was he going to manage that? Reading further, the cloud removal service was being aimed at holiday resorts, wedding couples and village fetes and other events of a similar nature. In fact, the advert claimed that the sky was the limit in terms of the service on offer.

Holiday resorts like Blackpool had lost out to places abroad like Spain, Italy and France because of their better record of sunshine. If Blackpool and other British resorts could be guaranteed the same record they could triple the amount of business that they were currently doing. There was bound to be a take up of the idea in the world of British tourism, thought Cirrus.

Sporting events can often be weather-dependent and, here again, the service being offered by Vannin's had distinct advantages. Just think of the number of cricket matches that got called off each season and how frustrating that could be, and tennis was another example, although Wimbledon had taken costly steps to build a movable roof over its tennis courts. The thing was, not every sporting organisation could afford such expensive solutions. The more Cirrus read the advert the more potential the idea seemed to have.

It was always something of a disappointment when someone's wedding was blessed with rain or a deep overcast. Both tend to spoil photographic opportunities and when a lot of money has been involved setting up the perfect day it is not surprising that a lot of couples are marrying in places more likely to be guaranteed sunshine. This brought back to Cirrus the job he once did at Clitheroe which he now felt guilty about. Deliberately raining on someone's wedding was not something to be proud about.

Around the British Isles literally thousands of fetes of one form or another are organised and most rely on good weather for their success. It was one of those great British traditions to hold fetes or other events to raise money, entertain, and bring people together. From Lands End to John 'o' Groats, groups of well-meaning folk form organising committees to run these events and in many cases a whole year may be spent putting things together. To see it all spoiled by bad weather can be a heartbreaking experience and as Vannin's advert pointed out, it could be prevented by hiring in his cloud removers.

The advert was becoming much of a muchness thought Cirrus but he had to concede that it was a service that would probably prove most popular. The last activity to be described as a possible beneficiary of the service was air displays. They are extremely expensive to put on but are highly popular in the UK. How many times have organisers been forced to curtail the flying displays due to inclement weather? Clearly, this was another kind of event that might jump at the service being offered.

"Skipper, the Superintendant is on the phone for you."

Cirrus picked up the phone and bade Mr Spite good morning.

"Cirrus, have you seen the advert in the paper regarding cloud removing?"

"Yes I have."

"Well I think we need to talk about it so get yourself over to Wythenshawe as soon as you can."

"I'll be there tomorrow," said Cirrus, who could tell from his voice that he was concerned.

Seated in Mr Spite's office in the weather centre, Mr Spite invited the crew of the Nimbus to give him their thoughts on Vannin's Cloud Removal business. Puffy was first to respond.

"What if someone pays Vannin's to get rid of us? Where will we be then?"

"That's a very pertinent point Puffy. Damn it, I can't get used to calling you Puffy when your real name is Percival. Why couldn't you use Percy, it sounds much more masculine. Anyway don't answer that. There are more important things to talk about."

It was clear to all three of Wythenshawe's experts that considerable merit had to be attributed to the Manx company's service and it was duly noted that the company quoted the service as being cheap and affordable, easy to fix and terms could be arranged without difficulty.

"What do we know about this guy Vannin?" asked Mr Spite.

"Not much really except that he invented a cloud condenser. We had one fitted on the Nimbus if you remember, to take water from Grantown-on-Spey to Peel."

"Ah yes, I do remember. I think we better look into this. When all is said and done, making rain and other things is our business, and we don't want someone else muscling in."

How does it work?

A plan was hatched to get someone into Vannin's factory in Peel to try and find out exactly what was going on. Mr Spite carefully considered who he should approach to do the job and eventually concluded that Henry Black would be the ideal person. Henry had recently lost his skipper and was out of cloud work. When approached, Henry jumped at the chance of doing something.

Henry travelled to the Isle-of-Man and got himself some cheap accommodation in Peel before making enquiries about work. As luck would have it, Vannin's needed a cleaner and Henry managed to get the job. He discreetly observed what was going on and noted snippets of conversation that he heard, but the breakthrough occurred when he worked late one evening. Tarpaulins covered a large object in one corner of the factory and when they were removed he was shocked by what he saw. The cloud machine Drip, like its owner, Arthur Treadmill, had been suspended for six months but here it was. Henry hid himself when he heard footsteps coming nearer and in due course he spotted Arthur and his Flight Engineer, Larry Oliver. The lights inside the factory were switched off and some large doors opened. The Drip was pushed out into the night and with the crew onboard it ascended into the darkness. Henry couldn't take the risk of being spotted but he knew enough already and he decided to head back to Wythenshawe as fast as he could.

Mr Spite was both amazed and disappointed to learn that one of his cloud crews was doing work whilst suspended but also doing work that could drastically affect Wythenshawe's operation. He decided that Arthur Treadmill and Larry Oliver should be brought back to Wythenshawe for questioning. Mr Spite had connections in the Police Force and in due course the crew of the Drip was brought back to face a grilling.

Cirrus and Puffy were both present at the interrogation that Arthur and Larry were about to be subjected to by Mr Spite. They complied fully, having been informed as to what could become of themselves if they resisted, and information flowed from them about the Manx-based cloud removers.

"It was like this Mr Spite," began Arthur. "They installed the cloud condenser equipment aboard the Drip using a local plumbing firm."

"A bloody plumber! That would make your insurance cover null and void," exclaimed Mr Spite who went on, "Only Black, Black & Blackemore's are permitted to make any changes to your machine, don't you realise that?"

"I do Mr Spite, but being suspended, I could hardly go to them. The cloud would be out of the bag, so to speak."

"So let me sum up before we go any further. You were operating whilst under suspension and with your insurance null and void."

"That's right Mr Spite," answered Arthur, who was now well aware that he was in deep trouble.

"Now what I want you to tell me, is how Vannin's plan to make the sky cloud-free."

This appeared to be a stumbling block. Both Arthur and Larry looked at each other but remained silent. Mr Spite repeated the question but again elicited no response.

"I can see we have a problem here," said Mr Spite. "In that case you leave me with no option."

Goldilocks was called into the office and instructed to tell Josh Harrop to make his way here. Josh had a fearsome reputation. He had in a previous life been a boxer of some notoriety, and legend had it that he had never been beaten. His notoriety was going before him and the crew of the Drip were evidently strained and the strain was noticeable in the way they were ringing their hands, and beads of sweat appeared on their brows.

After several minutes of tense silence, Josh was ushered into the office and was immediately met with the sudden capitulation of both interreges.

"Ok Mr Spite, Ok! We will tell you all we know," said an agitated Larry.

"What we do is go out at night and fly into the cloud that we have to remove. We switch the condenser on and the cloud gets sucked in through the four grill-covered orifices fitted along the sides of the Drip. It's a bit like a vacuum cleaner really. The condenser condenses the cloud vapour, turning it into water which we store in the machine's saddle tanks. We freeze some of it and store it as ice in our refrigerators. Then we go and rain somewhere to get rid of it and go back and suck another in."

"How many clouds can you suck up at one go?"

"Well, as you know, our machines when fully loaded can store water and ice, 4,000,000 gallons to be precise, and we can make a Manchester Black out of that and that's the largest cloud you can get. That means that at one suck we can swallow a Manchester Black or several other clouds like a Cumberland Grey or a Westmorland White, depending on how big they are."

"But it would take some time to clear a full sky with just one cloud remover," commented Mr Spite.

"Vannin's plan to recruit a fleet of cloud removers and fit them all with condensers and then use the fleet to clear the sky."

All very ingenious thought Mr Spite. He was not only worried about what he was hearing but also, to some degree, in admiration of the concept.

"I assume that your machines go out naked to do the job so when do you do it?"

"That's right, we do go out naked. There would be no point in creating our own cloud and then sucking it away, that would be achieving nothing, so we go out naked at night and do the cloud removing in the dark."

"That must limit your ability to clear the sky?"

"It is a limitation at present. We can do it with a large fleet of cloud removers but that bangs up the cost."

Up to this point Larry had done all the talking but now Arthur took up explaining the research that was currently underway.

"It would make the operation more versatile if we could clear clouds in daylight and that's what's being worked on right now. So far Vannin's have tried by fitting a drogue to the Drip. It's like a trailing hose that can be let out quite a distance. At the end of the drogue is a bell-like basket into which a cloud can be sucked. The Drip can go off into the sky in the middle of its own cloud and trail its hose so that it trails outside its own vapour. Then you can suck up other clouds."

Larry went on to explain some of the difficulties that they were experiencing with this technique at present.

"The trouble is, we have to overtake a cloud to do this in order to suck it up and that's not always possible. We have been trying a technique that involves positioning our cloud over the top of another and lowering the drogue into it. The problem we have found is that we need to put a weight on the end of the drogue to keep it perpendicular but the weight forces us down as well, so for the moment that's still ongoing."

This was all fascinating stuff and as far as Mr Spite was aware it was all legal. Where should he go from here, he thought.

Fleet volunteers

Vannin's had not attempted to recruit cloud machine owners to create its fleet of cloud removers other than Arthur Treadmill, but in his case it had been more clandestine than recruitment. It was, however, fast approaching the time that they did so. Discussions took place to establish how many cloud machines would be required to establish the fleet that would be needed and then, on how to acquire them.

After much debating, a decision was reached that the fleet should consist of ten machines but the method of recruitment took longer still to determine. Advertising in newspapers or in the Monthly Downpour would probably bring Vannin's into conflict with Wythenshawe Weather Centre and so it was decided that a word of mouth approach would be more appropriate.

"Now look here Treadmill," said Mr Vannin looking Arthur straight in the eye. "I want you to pick out ten of your colleagues at Wythenshawe who could be persuaded to come and join us here at Peel."

"That might not be easy Mr Vannin. The work at Wythenshawe is regular and established, not like here. My colleagues may be reluctant to leave. What do I say to them?"

"Look here Treadmill, don't be such a wet lettuce. You can tell them that this is the future for cloud machines. It won't be long before all the natural clouds have been removed from the sky and the only ones anyone will ever see in the future will be those hired from us. This is a progressive cloud company and places like Wythenshawe will be history. Anyway, if they don't tell Wythenshawe what they are doing, they can always go back. Is that clear enough for you?"

"Yes Mr Vannin."

Arthur pondered as to what his next move should be and in the end he decided to go straight to Mr Spite and tell him about the latest development.

"I think our best approach to this is for me to pick ten crews and brief them," said Mr Spite.

"You leave this to me and I will get back to you."

"Very well Mr Spite," and with that Arthur returned to the Isle-of-Man feeling relieved that Wythenshawe was sorting it out.

Cirrus was enjoying the company of Abigail in his Slaidburn home as Puffy, with the help of the lady in his life, arrived with morning coffee.

"I have a message for you, skipper, from Mr Spite. He wants you to ring him. He says it's urgent."

"Thanks Puffy, I'll give him a call."

"Ah, thanks for ringing Cirrus. I have something I want to talk to you about but I want to do it here at Wythenshawe. Can you get over?"

"You mean today?"

"Yes, if possible and ask Abigail to come as well will you?"

How did Mr Spite know that Abigail was here in the first place, thought Cirrus, not realising that their relationship was being followed with great interest by their colleagues?

When Cirrus and Abigail arrived at Wythenshawe they where directed to the conference room where they met eight other cloud machine owners and they all exchanged greetings before Mr Spite arrived.

"I have asked you all here today to tell you about a new development in the cloud world that may have big implications for us here at Wythenshawe."

Mr Spite went on tell the ten skippers everything he had been told by Arthur Treadmill as well as the details included in the newspaper advertisement.

"Where do we come into all this?" asked Windy Blower.

"Vannin's want to create a fleet of ten machines and I want you lot to be the volunteers. This way we can find out exactly what is happening and then take whatever action is appropriate. Are you up for it?"

The ten skippers looked at each other and, after one or two comments, unanimously agreed. It would be something new and different. Cloud removals instead of creations, that was different!

"What about our insurance cover Mr Spite? Doing this kind of work for a private firm and having a modification carried out on our machines by a non-registered company could affect our cover."

"That's a good point, leave it with me and I will get it sorted."

The details of the ten volunteers were passed on to Arthur Treadmill and he took them to his new boss, Mr Vannin.

"Good show Treadmill. I told you they would be interested if you gave them the right story. Now we'd better get them over here so that I can meet them."

A week later the ten volunteers arrived in the Isle-of-Man to be met by Arthur who took them to Peel. They entered the factory that belonged to Mr Vannin but were surprised at the sign outside which read, The Peel Wine and Spirits Company.

Once inside they met Mr Vannin who explained what his plan was. He then went on to describe the details of the modification that would be done to their cloud machines in order that they could become cloud removers.

"As soon as the modification is done you can learn how to use it and then we will be open for business."

"Have you got any work lined up yet?"

"I have had several enquiries and there are one or two things in the pipeline."

"What about pay? How will we be paid?"

"I won't pay you a salary. Instead, I will pay you for each cloud you remove on a sliding scale."

"What's the sliding scale?"

"I will pay you £25 for the removal of a Westmorland White, £50 for a Cumberland Grey, £75 for a Manchester Black and if it's a layer of Stratus £100 to each remover involved."

A few more details were made clear and then the ten owners had to sign a form including the name of their cloud machines which consisted of, the Nimbus, Flier, Dismal, Spitting, Hurricane, Softly Blows, Astro, Discovery, Skylark and Stormlark. With these formalities completed, everyone departed for Wythenshawe to collect their machines.

Moving home

The ten cloud machine owners about to become cloud removers agreed to depart Wythenshawe in two batches of five in order that nothing could be seen as odd by their many colleagues. The first batch consisted of the Nimbus, Flier, Dismal, Spitting and Hurricane. The five crews arrived early in the day to check out their machines, refuel them and take provisions on board. It was not often that so many machines could be seen at the same time in Wythenshawe's huge hangar. Later in the day, when darkness was approaching, they boarded their craft and started their fan duct motors. The huge Wythenshawe hangar doors started to open and the interior lights dimmed before finally going out. Each machine taxied out onto the concrete apron before stopping for a final instrument check. Identification beacons were switched on before radio contact was made with Wythenshawe control. With clearance given, the five machines ascended vertically into the night sky and continued until they reached an altitude of five thousand feet and then hovered momentarily.

Cirrus in the Nimbus instructed his Flight Engineer, Puffy, to contact the other four craft and give them the heading he had worked out to get them to the Isle-of-Man. Once that had been done, all five machines departed Wythenshawe's air space and headed North West for their destination. The first part of the flight on this cloudless night took them over Rivington Pike and Preston before reaching Fleetwood. Many twinkling lights could be observed below them but once Fleetwood was left behind it was a different story. Over the Irish Sea it seemed there was nothing but the dark surface of a flat sea. In due course, twinkling lights ahead on their port side were the first indication that they were nearing the Isle-of-Man. As they got nearer many of the lights had been extinguished which was a sure sign that many of the island's inhabitants had turned in for the night.

A slight alteration to course was made as they came abeam Douglas and they headed north until Ramsey was reached, at which point they headed west to cross the island's coast to reach the old airfield at Jurby. This old RAF Station would be their new home whilst working for Vannin. There was sufficient moonlight to allow the skippers of each craft to see the landing spot allocated to them outside the largest of the many hangars here, and they got back down without any incident. Ground staff guided them into the large hangar and their respective parking places using illuminated batons. Once parked, the hangar doors closed and the lights came on.

Each crew switched off their fan duct motors and grabbed their bags to depart and then made their way to the crafts exit door. Once out of their machines the five crews momentarily gathered to share their thoughts about the flight across and then they where greeted by Arthur Treadmill who escorted them to where they would be living.

There was not much left of the accommodation sites that had been built for the RAF during the Second World War but the temporary structure of the old Officer's Mess had stood the test of time and this would now be host to a new group of fliers who, it must be said, flew very different kinds of machines than their RAF forebears.

Each of the ten crew members had a room to themselves each with its own toilet and washing facilities. They would share a dining room and a very atmospheric Mess. Lots of RAF memorabilia covered the walls and it had a special feel about it. With all meals provided and a laundry service available, the crew members felt that this had all the ingredients of an enjoyable stay.

The remaining five craft, the Softly Blows, Astro, Discovery, Skylark and Stormlark arrived twenty four-hours later and the crews joined those that had arrived earlier in the Mess for a celebratory drink, and Arthur Treadmill and his Flight Engineer Larry Oliver joined them. Cirrus was most pleased that Abigail was involved in the same job and so was Puffy in the knowledge that Carol was involved too. If one forgot about the task in hand there would be a temptation to think that it was like a group holiday but there was a serious side to all this and they would be getting to know about it very soon.

Trying it out

The ten cloud machine crews were assembled in the large hangar at Jurby airfield and Mr Vannin arrived to brief them on what was about to happen.

"Good morning everybody! I'm glad to see that you are all here. What is about to happen is quite simple. First, we must modify your machines by installing the cloud condenser equipment which is vital for the jobs you will eventually undertake. I have been told that it will take a week to carry out the work and it will be done here at Jurby. Once your machines have been modified, you will need to go off and try it on yourself and when you have mastered your own disappearing act you can go off and try it on the real stuff."

Before anyone could ask any questions Mr Vannin left, leaving the twenty crew members a little mystified as to what they should do now. Fortunately Arthur Treadmill turned up to take over from where Mr Vannin had left off.

"You can all take the week off and explore the island whilst your machines are modified but before you go just make sure that the access doors on your machines are left open and the access ladders are extended. Blimps engineers will need access to do the modifications."

What a bonus, the crews thought, a holiday all thrown in! This job was already a lot more enjoyable than what they had been doing before and they rapidly dispersed to make their own plans. This was a wonderful opportunity for Cirrus and Puffy to cement their relationships with Abigail and Carol and for the moment cloud removals was the last thing on their minds.

The engineers from Blimps the Plumbers in Ramsey descended on Jurby en masse to modify the ten cloud machines and they worked round the clock to get the job finished. They may not have been aeronautical engineers but they were good with a hammer and wrench and made easy meat of the job. Outwardly the only change was the appearance of two fairly large grill-covered holes along each side of each machine. These were the holes into which a cloud would be sucked. Internally, a lot of pipes had been plumbed in to take the sucked-in cloud to the condenser which condensed the cloud vapour into water before it left by another lot of pipes to be stored in the craft's saddle tanks. Some of the condensed cloud would be sent to the craft's refrigerators to be stored as ice.

Once the machines had been modified they were inspected by Mr Blimp and other than the damage to the crafts' paintwork, both externally and internally, he was satisfied with what his engineers had accomplished. The paintwork was rapidly restored to its original condition and it was now time to call back the crews to get their training underway.

Cirrus and Abigail had spent a romantic week together exploring the island and had visited Douglas, Castletown, Port Erin, Peel and Ramsey. They had travelled on trains and trams and had been to a couple of concerts in Douglas, but the most enjoyable part was walking arm in arm together at the various places they had been to. Cirrus fell in love with Abigail in the Isle-of-Man and it was the finest moment of his life. The feeling was mutual. Puffy and Carol on the other hand, well they had a great time too, and the intervals between necking sessions got longer as their passion started to mature into a feeling of strong mutual contentment. Sharing each other's company was getting just as good as the kissing, and in Puffy's case that was saying something. All four were a little disappointed when it was time to return to work.

Arthur showed each crew what had been done to their machine and indicated the position of the new switches on the Flight Engineer's panel.

"Well it's up to you now to go out and test it on yourself and when you are happy with it, let me know and we will move on to the next stage of your training."

The ten crews were then left to their own resources to get on with it.

"I think we will try it out tonight Puffy," said Cirrus, and the two of them set about checking over the Nimbus making sure that it was fuelled and that some provisions were on board.

As the evening fell, Cirrus and Puffy made a final check before starting the four fan duct motors and then, giving a thumbs up through the cockpit window to one of Vannin's men, the lights in the hangar went out and the doors opened. The Nimbus emerged from the hangar into the night sky and ascended into the darkness before heading west over the Irish Sea. When they had got about half way to Northern Ireland, Cirrus brought the Nimbus to the hover and instructed Puffy to atomise 4,000,000 gallons of water into a Westmorland White cloud. Normally this type of cloud would be used to decorate a blue sky and enhance its beauty but in the night this was of no consequence, being almost invisible to the naked eye. Once they had created their own cloud, it was necessary to use the craft's TV Camera to provide an image of the outside world on the pop-up screen on the flight deck.

Now for the big test, thought both crew members of the Nimbus!

"Puffy, just check that our water tanks are empty and also that our fridges are free of ice will you?"

"Aye, aye skipper."

A few moments passed and then Puffy got back to him.

"Water tanks empty and refrigerators free from ice skipper."

"Thanks Puffy. Condense our cloud then. Let's see what happens."

With that Puffy operated the appropriate switches and the process began. Although it wasn't visible, the Westmorland White was rapidly decreasing in size as it disappeared into the four side-mounted holes, only to reappear in the craft's water tanks and refrigerators. The dials on the Flight Engineer's panel illustrated the rate at which their cloud was being turned into water and ice.

The picture on the TV screen took on a sudden degree of extra clarity as their cloud completely vanished and all the dials on Puffy's control panel showed that all the water tanks and all the refrigerators were full.

"Well bless my soul, it really works well!" said Cirrus.

"What do we do now skipper?" asked Puffy.

"Well this is where, if we were doing a job, we would take all our water and ice and get rid of it and the only way we can do that is to make a cloud and rain. Switch on our evaporators and we can convert our water back to cloud."

"What about the ice skipper?"

"Switch on the sublimator and we can make that into cloud as well."

The two crew watched the dials on Puffy's control panel unwind and as they did so a cloud was recreated around the Nimbus. When all the dials registered empty, Cirrus gave the order to rain and it did until the cloud had completely disappeared again.

"Well it works but what a palaver," remarked Cirrus, and the Nimbus set off home for Jurby after a good night's work.

When all the crews got together in the old Officers' Mess they exchanged stories about their experiences and it soon became evident that the new equipment installed on their machines had functioned well. There was also general agreement that the process was a bit long-winded what with sucking up a cloud, taking it way, remaking it and then raining it off, but it did work so what next? They did not have long to wait to find out. Arthur was back on the scene and told them that they'd better get out and try it on the real thing and tomorrow night might not be a bad time according to the weather forecast.

The following night all ten machines got airborne to practise the art of removing a cloud. Each cloud machine picked a natural cloud in the moonlight and all went well except for the Dismal and the Stormlark who both chose the same one. A heated argument took place over the radio waves before any agreement was reached but it was all plain cloud-removing after that. Sucking up a natural cloud was no more difficult than sucking up your own, you simply flew inside one and switched your equipment on and hey presto, it was gone. Take it away as water and ice, recreate it, rain, and that was the end of life for one cloud. What could be simpler?

Back in the Officers' Mess the crews swopped tales and once again there was general agreement that everything had worked just fine. It was agreed however, that it had been simpler taking off and flying naked straight into a natural cloud and vacuuming it up to be taken away and dumped somewhere as rain.

Just as everyone was getting relaxed and beginning to enjoy themselves Arthur burst in.

"Just heard from the Met Office that tomorrow night we will be covered by a layer of stratus cloud and that means it will be a golden opportunity to practise working as a team to remove it. Your training will be complete then."

"Arthur why don't you go and fall in a river?" shouted someone who disliked having his social time interrupted.

The following night was particularly dark as the layer of stratus stretched as far as could be seen, which in this light was not far at all. The ten machines got airborne and ascended to an agreed height which took them inside the cloud. They spread out so that there was half a mile between them. This was not easy to do inside a cloud but Cirrus took command and, using his Plan Position Indicator, he gave instructions to each cloud remover in turn to move to a particular set of co-ordinates until they formed a line on his PPI screen. Then they all switched their condensers on and waited for the stratus to be collectively removed and it worked a treat.

"By gum Alice, the forecasters have got it wrong tonight!"

"How do you mean Bert?"

"Well they said we would be covered with cloud tonight but if you go outside it's a clear night sky. You can see stars in every direction."

"Go on with you Bert!"

"I'm telling you Alice, it's true!"

Bert and Alice were not the only Manx folk thinking that the forecasters had got it wrong tonight.

Mr Vannin made an appearance the following day and congratulated everyone on the completion of their training. He told them that he was now in a position to positively accept work and they should all ensure that they were ready to fly into action.

Cirrus reported back to Mr Spite on everything that had transpired and warned him that they were now ready to embark on real cloud-removing work. Mr Spite felt quite frustrated at the way things were panning out but as yet he had no option but to wait and see how things developed.

All day sunshine

Blackpool was the first place to take advantage of Vannin's Cloud Removals. Each year they promoted a most popular bathing beauties competition which in recent years had been marred by bad weather. The possibility of guaranteeing a day of sunshine could not be resisted and although it was expensive to arrange, it might be worth it, especially if the guarantee was advertised.

Back in Jurby, the ten cloud machine crews had a briefing regarding the forthcoming operation. The bathing beauty contest would be held in an afternoon and this highlighted the first problem with the current way things had to be done. In order to protect their anonymity they had to operate at night and hence they would have to work out where, if any, the clouds would be that needed removing before they reached Blackpool at the contest time. That was not an easy job to do. The wind is somewhat uncanny and although you think you can predict its direction and strength, both can change. There was clearly a risk involved.

For the moment, weather charts were carefully analysed and it was apparent that there was a cloud belt heading for Blackpool propelled by a ten knot south westerly wind and its position in the very early hours of the contest day was plotted.

"Gentlemen, that's where we need to intercept the cloud belt and remove it," said Cirrus pointing to a position just west of the Isle of Anglesey. "We need to get airborne as soon as it gets dark and head out to our intercept position and get on with the job."

In the darkness of the night, ten naked cloud removing machines headed out to meet the cloud belt that they had to remove and they fanned out into a line and spaced themselves one mile apart from each other using the PPI as previously practised. It wasn't long before they could see the cloud belt approaching them and it consisted of broken cloud running to their left and right as far as they could see using their TV camera. This presented problem number two! There simply weren't enough of them to remove the whole cloud belt. They would have to carve a niche in that part of the belt that would pass over Blackpool but which part would that be?

Cirrus Cumulus could see that there was a lot more to this cloud removal business than had been worked out. He studied his charts and made a quick decision as to where the ten cloud removers should concentrate and then issued instructions. It was a calculated guess but that was the best he could do. Cloud condensers were activated and soon a whole armada of natural clouds were being vacuumed out of the sky. The ten machines remained in a stationary line and it would have been quite strange to see, if that was possible in the dark, a wide carpet of clouds being blown north east having what looked like a channel being cut out of it as it progressed past the Isle of Anglesey.

Eventually, the cloud belt now split in two continued its journey, leaving ten cloud machines behind heavily laden with water and ice. With the departure of the cloud belt, Cirrus gave the order to stand fast, make clouds and rain. And that's exactly what they did before heading back to Jurby. But by now it was daylight and they would have a long wait before darkness fell again. They hovered off the west coast of the Isle-of-Man just out of sight of land until it was dark and then went in to land.

Once inside the large hangar at Jurby and the doors had been closed and the lights switched on, Mr Vannin could be seen waiting for them and he didn't look too pleased.

"What the dickens went on up there?" he barked at the crews as they gathered around him. Cirrus explained that because there were not enough of them they had had to carve a channel in the cloud belt but it had not been possible to know exactly where, so they had taken a calculated guess.

"Well you calculated wrong. Blackpool was covered by broken clouds and Southport had a clear day. The beauty contest organisers are furious and are threatening not to pay us and if I don't get paid then neither do you."

With that Mr Vannin stormed off.

Later in the Mess the crews got to talking about the problems they had encountered with the operation and at the end of it they concluded that there needed to be far more of them to do this kind of work, Nature's cloud belts covered many nautical miles, far too many to be removed by ten cloud machines. It was also concluded that it would have been better to intercept the cloud belt nearer to the time of the contest. That would take care of any wind changes that would alter its course, but that in turn would require the cloud removers to be cloud-covered themselves, and the technique of cloud removing in this mode had not yet been perfected. To add to what was turning out to be a frustrating day, the threat of not being paid for what they thought was no fault of their own was not going down well, but at least a drink in the Mess was.

Protecting a great event

The world's greatest spectacle of Brass Bands descends on a collection of villages around Tameside and Saddleworth in the North West of England annually to contest. Each village organises its own competition and bands work their way around from one to another in order to qualify for overall awards which are an additional incentive. It is not unusual for sixty bands to play in one village and this wonderful spectacle is free to enjoy. The collection of village contests take place on a Friday evening and bad weather had had an impact on occasions, much to the disappointment of the many organising committees who spend a full year planning for the big day. This was an event that would certainly benefit from a guarantee of dry conditions and Vannin's got the contract to ensure that that is what the village committees got.

At Jurby, Mr Vannin briefed the ten cloud machine crews on the latest operation and then read them the riot act on what would happen if they got it wrong, and then hastily left before they could put any questions to him.

"Cirrus, I think you are the one to plan our method of approach for this job. You are the only one skilled enough to do it," said Wally, the skipper of the Discovery.

Cirrus was flattered by Wally's comments but was concerned about the possible reaction of his colleagues if it didn't go right.

"Don't worry about a thing Cirrus. If this operation goes wrong we all know it will not be down to any planning that you do," said Albertino.

Reassured, Cirrus mused on the challenge. He began by looking at the location of all the villages situated to the east of Manchester on a line running north to south. The most northerly village was almost thirty miles from the most southerly and that presented a challenge in itself. How could ten cloud removers claw a channel in cloud thirty miles wide? Next he looked at the time of the contests. They started at 4-00pm and could go on until midnight. Any channel being carved out of approaching cloud, assuming there was going to be any, would have to last for eight hours and that was another immense challenge.

Having taken a look at what was required, Cirrus turned his attention to the weather forecast and it couldn't have been worse. The forecast predicted rain-bearing clouds for the whole day carried on a westerly wind at fifteen knots.

"What's up skipper?" asked Puffy.

"You might well ask. It's going to rain all day and there is no end in sight for over twenty-four hours. I'm blowed if we can accomplish this job."

Once Cirrus had finished his plan he got his colleagues together and explained what he intended.

"We will get airborne tonight and take up a position ten nautical miles west of Southport. We will remain in that position until 10-00pm on Friday. We will each be one nautical mile apart so that we can create a cloud-free channel ten miles wide."

"But don't we need it thirty miles wide?" asked Abigail.

"Yes we do but that's not achievable with just ten machines. Anyway, carrying on: the wind is a westerly at fifteen knots and our position over the Irish Sea is forty-five nautical miles from the contest location. That means that it will take clouds three hours to reach the area from where we will be. The contests start at 4-00pm so if we start removing clouds at 1-00pm then a clear spell will reach the contest location by 4-00pm."

"By gum Cirrus, you can certainly plan things alright," remarked Sunny.

It wasn't all going to be plain cloud removing thought Cirrus but he wasn't going to enlarge on things at this stage.

In due course the ten machines departed Jurby in the darkness of night and headed for their operating position over the Irish Sea, ten nautical miles west of Southport. On arrival they hovered and waited for the arrival of nature's armada of rain-bearing clouds and when they saw it approaching from the west it stretched north and south further than the eye could see and cast a dark shadow on the surface of the sea below it. Cirrus had got his colleagues to hover at five thousand feet and at one mile intervals. The crews felt somewhat overawed as they viewed nature's cloud army progressing steadily towards them. It was most eerie as the progressing clouds swallowed them into their misty interiors. The outside world was no longer visible through the cockpit windows of the cloud machines and peripheral vision was now provided by the pop-up TV screen. Although they couldn't see it, each machine was now immersed in clouds on the move and which would continue for over twenty-four hours if they remained there. Being 11-00am in the morning, they would have to wait for another two hours before they would switch on their condensers and start cloud removing.

Two hours hovering in clouds on the move seemed like an eternity and everyone was much relieved when Cirrus gave the order to start cloud removing. It was remarkable how a ten nautical mile wide channel of clear sky started to be carved out of the layer of nature's sky carpet and anyone down below would have had a real spectacle to observe. Carving the channel started at 1-00pm and lasted for one hour, by which time each machine was full to capacity with water and ice. At 2-00pm Cirrus gave the order to start making cloud and then create a monsoon to get rid of what they were storing. Doing it in this way, each machine could be ready again to cloud remove in thirty minutes. During the thirty minutes that this was taking place no channel was being carved in nature's cloud carpet. At 2-30pm cloud removal began again and this sequence of events was repeated every ninety minutes until 10-00pm at which time each cloud machine was naked and empty and left the scene for Jurby.

Greenfield is roughly in the middle of the north south line of villages holding a contest and had been experiencing continuous rain for a couple of hours as the start time approached. It was with great relief that a clear sky was observed approaching and its arrival coincided with the first Brass Band starting off on its march down the main street, playing with great gusto as it did so. The audience lining the route applauded with enthusiasm as the first band (Greenfield Band, who else could it be?) marched along with a spring in its step. The sight of four tubas at its head was always a sight to behold and there would be another sixty bands to follow before the night was out, each one preceded by a youngster bearing a sign with name of the band and the name of the march it was playing.

The first hour at Greenfield and several other villages situated roughly in the centre of the contest territory passed under a cloud free sky, but at 5-00pm that changed to rain for thirty minutes and then it was back to blue sky again. The contest was subjected to thirty minute sessions of rain at hourly intervals all evening until it was all over, but at least they had done better than those villages to the north and south who had been subjected to continuous rain all evening.

The aftermath

The organising committees from the various villages were not impressed with what Vannin's Cloud Removers had achieved. It had cost them an arm and a leg and there had been no benefit whatsoever in many locations, and those that had experienced a benefit were still not totally rain-free on the day. A vote was taken and it was unanimously agreed that no payment should be made to the Manx company and they were to be informed that no further business would be going their way in the future.

Mr Vannin didn't speak to the crews of the cloud machines at Jurby; he was in too bad a mood. He got Arthur to deliver the news to them and they gathered in the old Officers' Mess.

"Mr Vannin has asked me to tell you that you are all fired and are to depart Jurby as soon as you can."

"What reason has he given for firing us?"

"He reckons you botched the Brass Band contest job and he got no pay for it."

"There are good reasons why the job couldn't be done. There simply were not enough of us and secondly, we need to be able to operate during the day and much closer to the locations that want a cloud-free environment," said Cirrus.

"That may be so and I think Mr Vannin knows that but he has decided to throw the towel in. The cost involved getting together an armada of cloud machines would make the whole business non-viable so he's packing it all in."

"What about paying us?"

"You won't be getting anything. You will have to settle for the free food and accommodation you have had."

Arthur departed and left the crews chatting to each other. The collapse of the cloud removal business had come as no surprise; they had fully expected it after the last two jobs. The loss of earnings was no issue either; Mr Spite had funded them all to be here in order to gain an accurate picture as to what was going on. Both Cirrus and Puffy had benefitted in a romantic fashion and had no complaints about their visit to the Isle-of-Man, and that went for Abigail and Carol too.

In Wythenshawe Weather Centre Mr Spite was greatly relieved to hear the news about Vannin's Cloud Removers but, like Cirrus, not really surprised. He summed the whole business up as a clear case of the sheer size of nature proving too much to be harnessed. The future would continue playing to nature's whims, clouds and all!

THE LATEST FROM DEEPER SALFORD

At home in Slaidburn

It was great to take a rest after the mad Vannin business and Cirrus, together with his companion Puffy, were both enjoying getting the garden at their Slaidburn home up to scratch. Puffy was the gardener of the two; Cirrus was more of a labourer. It fell to him to give the lawn a weekly 'short back and sides' and to hoe the borders, checking at the same time that flowers such as daffodils or tulips were all in neat regimental lines. There were many leaves to collect up around the place and a compost heap to keep in a manageable state. Puffy was the one with the green fingers and it was he who looked after the greenhouse and potted various plants. He also did the pruning of the roses and trees. The pair of them made a good gardening partnership and they kept the place generally looking good, although it was sometimes a bit of a challenge, especially when a weather job had kept them away for some time.

There never seemed to be any end to gardening and home repairs. No sooner had the crew of the Nimbus sorted out one job than another cropped up. Currently the door hinges on the garage needed attention. One of the doors was hard to open and the telephone was acting up. It would not have been so bad if Cirrus had not just had to have a puncture repaired on one of his car wheels. There was never a dull moment when it came to repair jobs.

When not involved with gardening or house repairs, Cirrus spent a fair amount of his time ensuring that an appropriate amount of memorabilia was on display in his home to paint an accurate picture of his life. He planned to leave it all to someone but that was a problem, who would he leave his history to? That was a question he tended to put to one side. For now, the important thing was to ensure that lots of evidence of him being here was left for someone and the evidence took on a number of different forms. On the walls were a number of photographs of his mother and father, Puffy and of course himself. There were photos of his cloud machine, with and without cloud, although it has to be said that with cloud there was little evidence of the Nimbus. There were photos of various types of clouds, but Westmorland Whites, Cumberland Greys and Manchester Blacks were the most prominent. Wythenshawe Weather Centre was on show amongst the collection that had by now spread to every room in the house.

It wasn't just photos that festooned the walls of the Slaidburn home; there were also framed course certificates and various qualifications along with his membership of The Guild of Cloud-Owners'. Pride of place however, went to his C.D.M. (Cloud Defence Medal) which was mounted above the fireplace in his lounge.

Cirrus had always been a keen model builder and umpteen examples could be found around the house, all made from plastic kits that came from around the world. He was particularly proud of the model of the Nimbus which had a removable top that revealed the interior details. His current modelling interest revolved around his second home in Ballyhalbert which was built on an old military airfield. The Royal Air Force and the Royal Navy had both used Ballyhalbert airfield in its short life of four years but, during that time, some thirty to forty different kinds of aircraft had operated from there. Cirrus was busy creating a collection of models that represented those historical times, and his latest was a Dominie aircraft which he had acquired from a French kit- maker.

The most important record of Cirrus and his work was without doubt the book that sat on top of his lounge sideboard, titled 'Nimbus'. This was almost like an illustrated diary that recorded all the things he and Puffy had done over the years, and new entries were made on a regular basis and photos, maps and charts added when it was felt necessary. Taking a look at the book, Cirrus realised that there were a couple of omissions.

"Puffy, did you realise that we haven't entered anything about the Vannin job in our memoirs book?"

"We didn't mention the naming of the house either," remarked Puffy.

"That's a good point. We can't let a name like Aurora Cloudealis go unrecorded."

Cirrus set to work on the book and then suddenly realised something.

"You know Puffy; I must arrange for Black, Black & Blakemore's to remove that damn cloud condenser that Vannin had fitted. Give them a ring will you and organise a date?"

Typical, thought Puffy. The skipper is always having ideas but when it comes to sorting them it's me that always gets the job.

Cirrus returned to making fresh entries in the book headed 'Nimbus' and as he did so he decided to play some background music. He took a Cd of Leyland Band from a shelf and placed it in his Cd player. Brass Bands were a great favourite of his and when the Band began by playing Kenneth Alford's arrangement of that great march 'Imperial Echoes' he slipped into his own private world to experience the heart- warming feeling he always got when listening to a good band playing a good march. The same Cd had a number of tracks on it by his composer friend Lucy Pankhurst: 'Mr Sonnemans Unusual Solution' and 'St,Kildas Fling'. And when he heard them it brought back many memories of past events spanning more years than he cared to recall. The Nimbus had been to many places and done many things.

Puffy came into the lounge and broke the concentration of Cirrus.

"There's a screw missing from the house name board on the garden wall," he announced.

"I hadn't noticed," said Cirrus, who then carried on with his writing. Puffy meanwhile went off to see what he had in the way of screws.

The morning paper

Now for it, thought Puffy as the morning paper arrived late. After a good start to the day it could all change. If there was anything in the Daily Gloom that his skipper didn't like, and more than likely there would be, his mood would change and that usually meant trouble one way or another for him. A quick scan of the contents and Puffy decided that his best course of action would be to give the skipper his paper with a cup of coffee and then disappear into the shed at the back of the house. An hour later Puffy made his way back indoors and he spotted Cirrus pacing backwards and forwards in the lounge with his hands behind his back, rather like Napoleon used to do. He had to collect the dirty cup, so there was no point in debating with himself as to whether he should go into the lounge or not, and in he went.

"Those damn politicians of ours, they will be the ruin of this country."

Wait for it, thought Puffy, something has got him going.

"Just look at this," said Cirrus, pointing at some headline that Puffy stood no chance of reading before he got into full flow. "The Government are sending our forces to the border of Syria. Before you can say 'boo', they will be dragged into that country's civil war. Don't they think that we have had enough of fighting somebody else's war? Don't they understand that wherever we have sent our forces to fight and die, no good has come of it?"

There was a slight pause before Cirrus stepped into verbal action once more. "It's somewhat of an irony that on the day we find out that our forces are being sent to Syria some five thousand soldiers are being made redundant. Things like this seem at odds with each other and it does nothing for the reputation of the top man at the head of our forces to say that these redundancies will have no impact on our ability to defend ourselves. Poppycock! He's toeing the party line in order to keep his job."

The opinions of the captain of the Nimbus now moved to another issue spurred by today's Daily Gloom.

"I know that there is a lot of cheating going on in respect of our benefits system and I agree that things should be tightened up to stop it, but it is only small fry compared with tax evasion by the big multi-national companies and people with vast fortunes. Do you know Puffy that it has been estimated that seventy billion pounds of potential tax income fails to reach the national coffers as a result of tax evasion techniques? That's really big money compared with the one million pounds that it is estimated is wrongly paid to benefit cheats. The Government demonises the benefit cheats but says little about the tax evaders."

Blimey! thought Puffy. I wonder how long it's going to take the skipper to get things off his mind.

"This political shower running things keep harping on about the need to keep on the world's top stage as one of the main players. They say we can influence the world much better from there. Influence, influence, who do we influence anymore? The big multinational companies wield more influence than our politicians. They need to get real and stop thinking about their own self importance. If its wisdom they are after it might help if they had the experience of a proper job instead of being career politicians straight from Eton or Harrow."

Luckily, it looked as if Cirrus had exhausted his feelings about the general demise of his beloved country, and whilst Puffy may have shared some of his captain's views to a greater or lesser degree, he knew it would not be wise to say so. If he did it would only be a spur for him to carry on again.

"Did you enjoy your coffee skipper?"

"Ah, yes I did Puffy. I suppose you think I have been prattling on again don't you? I can always tell, you know, and you would be right of course. But you have to admit, the country is going down the pan."

Romance and all that

A new photo had appeared on the lounge wall and Puffy was a little surprised to see it. The photo was of Cirrus and Abigail walking arm in arm along the sea front at Douglas. That was not a surprise in itself but what was a surprise was that it was hanging in a place normally reserved for the things close to the heart of Cirrus, which up until that time had been entirely to do with weather-making. There must be something significant happening to his skipper, thought Puffy.

"Skipper can I ask you something rather personal?"

"What might that be? replied Cirrus.

"Is there something special between you and Abigail?"

Cirrus blushed. He was not good at coping with his personal feelings, at least not verbally.

"What makes you ask that Puffy?"

"I've seen the photo of you and Abigail that you have put on the wall and normally you only put stuff on there that is special to you."

"Well you might as well know, Abigail is special to me. I thought I was past that sort of thing but Abigail has proved that I was wrong. I have never felt this way in my life before and I'm trying to come to terms with it."

"Are you in love Cirrus?"

That was a pretty pointed question but it was time to face the truth, thought Cirrus.

"Yes I think I am in love with Abigail."

"And what about Abigail, is she in love with you?"

"I think she is."

"Have you told her that you are in love with her?"

No I haven't, I find it difficult to do that."

"Skipper I think you should because I think she's crazy about you."

Cirrus blushed again but he was most flattered at the same time.

"Why don't you invite her over here and tell her. I think she would be delighted to hear it."

"Puffy there are other things to think about before I do that."

"Such as?"

"If we got hitched what would we do for a place to live in, for a start?"

"You would live here. It's your place, your house and it's lovely and Abigail thinks it's great."

"But you and I have both shared this place for years Puffy. What would you do?"

"You don't worry about me skipper, I might get married myself one of these days."

"Are you and Carol contemplating something long term?"

"We might be, we just might be."

Cirrus retired to a quiet corner of the garden to think about the future and those most close to him. He had resigned himself to a permanent life of weather-making with his dear friend Puffy and to spending his remaining days at Slaidburn. He did not consider himself morbid, just realistic. His new relationship had put a question mark over his perceived future and he simply hadn't put a plan in place. He was seriously thinking what it would be like sharing a home with Abigail, but for the moment he couldn't face the idea of asking his faithful companion of many years to find another place to live. He would also need to think about what would happen in relation to his work. Making rain and other things was his business. He had been doing it with Puffy for many years and it was the only thing he really knew much about. For the moment there was a lot to think about but he did agree about one thing and that was that it was time to tell Abigail of his feelings for her, and he went back into the house to ring her.

"Hello Cirrus, how nice to hear from you."

"Abigail, I have something important to say to you and I wondered if you could come up to Slaidburn for a couple of days?"

"Oh, that sounds ominous Cirrus. The trouble is, I have a lot of work on at present. Just hang on and I will check my diary."

Cirrus began to wonder whether she was sidestepping him."

"I can call next Wednesday but I can only stay for a few hours. Is that enough or can you not just tell me over the phone now?"

"I don't want to tell you over the phone Abigail. Next Wednesday will be fine."

When the call had ended, Abigail was left wondering what it was that Cirrus would not say over the phone. She was a pretty shrewd lady and she already knew how Cirrus felt about her. Was he going to propose? She realised that Cirrus and Puffy had been companions for a long time and a very special bond existed between them. She respected that and had no intention of coming between the two of them, but she also knew she was in love with Cirrus and the existing impasse was not going to last forever. She looked forward to her next visit to Slaidburn with a great feeling of expectancy.

A couple of days later, Puffy and Cirrus took a drive into Lancaster and Cirrus left his faithful companion to visit a jeweller's shop. I wonder what that is all about, thought Puffy but he had an idea which made him a bit excited. Is he going to, he thought?

In due course, Cirrus re-emerged from the shop with a small parcel in his hand and a smile on his face.

"Right Puffy, let's get back to Slaidburn!"

On the journey back little was said until they reached Clitheroe, at which point Cirrus spoke.

"Abigail will be coming over next Wednesday and I would be most grateful if you would make a nice meal for us both. Oh, and get some flowers in as well."

"That's no problem skipper. Will she be staying overnight?"

"Unfortunately no, she has a lot of work on at present."

There the conversation ended but both men had their private thoughts to entertain them.

Wednesday arrived after what had been a few very long days of acute anxiety, mixed with a pending degree of excitement. Flowers abounded around the 'Aurora Cloudealis' and the kitchen was in a high state of readiness. The crew of the Nimbus worked feverishly to complete a whole host of small tasks to help create the right atmosphere, although only Cirrus knew exactly what was going to happen. At about 10-30am the phone rang.

"Skipper that was Abigail. She can't make it. She says something has cropped up but she will be in touch as soon as she can."

A new model

Cirrus had slipped into a mild bout of depression. It never lasted, but it was not nice to see him so downhearted. For a few days his mood didn't change and Puffy began to get a bit aggravated with it all. Fortunately the next edition of the Monthly Downpour contained something that just might snap him out of it and Puffy took it along into the lounge together with a cup of coffee and a bacon butty. Cirrus was very partial to Puffy's bacon butties so there was no point in missing out on an opportunity to try and bring him round.

"Captain, I think you will find something of interest in this latest edition," said Puffy, as he handed the copy of the monthly journal to Cirrus along with the coffee and bacon butty.

The delicious smell of the bacon took precedence and Cirrus got well into it before taking any interest in the periodical handed to him by his faithful engineer. What was Puffy on about? thought Cirrus as he started to scan through it. Nothing grabbed his attention to begin with and after a second look through he shouted to Puffy.

"Puffy, what did you see that you thought might interest me?"

"It's on page twenty-five skipper."

Cirrus turned to page twenty-five and spotted an article about a new cloud machine that had been developed by Black, Black & Blackemore's in deeper Salford.

The current cloud machine, the Nimbus, owned by Cirrus was getting on a bit now and was showing its age a little, so it was of particular interest to learn about a new model. Black, Black & Blackemore's had been designing and developing cloud machines since the early 1940s and was the sole manufacturer of these machines in the whole world. Strangely enough, there had never been any overseas sales but it was rumoured that certain members of the Government had made it their business over the years to tell prospective foreign buyers that the products manufactured in Salford were not worth buying. Although there was no hard evidence to support this notion, there was still a strong suspicion that it was true. When all was said and done, Governments had a track record of this kind of activity in the past.

Reading further, Cirrus was interested to learn that the new model looked, outwardly, the same as the Nimbus but it incorporated some important improvements. For a start, the fan duct motors installed were more fuel-efficient. They also delivered more power and they were cleaner, which meant that the exhaust contained less polluting gasses which in this day and age was most important. The extra fuel efficiency meant that they could go further on the same fuel and save on costs. The extra power was less important although there was the occasion when that bit extra was an advantage. In addition to the new engines, the new model had more modern communications equipment fitted and the navigation aids had been updated. Whilst all these things were good news, thought Cirrus, they were not world record-breaking improvements, but there was more to read and he continued on.

"Bloody hell Puffy! Come and listen to this."

Good, thought Puffy, something has captured the skipper's attention, and he hurried off to join him.

"Black, Black & Blackemore's have developed a new cloud machine."

"What's new about it skipper?"

"It's got new, more powerful and cleaner engines that are also more efficient. They have also got improved communications and navigation equipment." Cirrus then paused before going on in an excited fashion.

"You will never believe it but the new model can deliver both snow and hailstones. What about that?"

"That really is impressive skipper. Are there any more details?"

"Yes there are. It can deliver light snow, heavy snow or sleet for that matter and if it's hailstones that you require then it can deliver small ones or big ones. What do you think about that?"

It was abundantly clear that Cirrus had put his recent disappointment behind him and that he was now focusing on something else. It was not long before he was on the phone to his pal, Wally Lenticular, discussing the article. Wally shared his enthusiasm for a machine that could deliver snow and hailstones. It increased the versatility of their machines and widened their scope for work.

"There's a phone call for you skipper."

"Who is it?"

"It's Mr Spite from Wythenshawe Weather Centre."

"I'll take it; put him through."

"Is that you Cirrus?"

"Good morning Mr Spite, yes, this is Cirrus. What can I do for you?"

Have you seen the article in the Monthly Downpour about the latest model of cloud machine?"

"Yes I have and I think it sounds splendid."

"You know Cirrus, a machine that can produce snow and hailstones should be a great boost for our line of business. I have had lots of enquiries in the past and not been in a position to do anything about it."

"I have the same feeling and so does Wally Lenticular."

"I think you should get yourself off to Black, Black & Blackemore's showroom to take a look at it. If it's as good as the brochure says it is, perhaps you may consider buying one."

"I am interested, but the finances would have to be available," answered Cirrus.

"You go along to deeper Salford and have a good look at this new machine, Cirrus, and then we can talk finance between us," remarked Mr Spite.

An appointment was duly made to visit the Salford-based cloud machine builder and a visit was made to see his bank manager in order to check that his finances were substantial enough for him to afford any purchase he may wish to make. He also bore in mind Mr Spite's comments regarding possible financial assistance.

"Puffy, put into our diary will you that next week we are going to take a look at that new model at Black, Black & Blakemore's."

"Right oh skipper, will do!"

Down at the showroom

On the north bank of the Manchester Ship Canal, along a road now called Pacific Way, is the factory of the world's only cloud manufacturing business, namely, Black, Black & Blackemore's, which also has its own wharf. At the western end of Salford docks, it had an advantageous position and the wharf would have been ideal for shipping, making it easy to load new machines destined for places around the world. Alas, exports had not materialised and the wharf these days simply acted as a launch pad for machines being delivered to and from Wythenshawe Weather Centre. There had been talk about setting up a weather-making research centre at Llanbedr in Wales but so far that had not happened and the hoped-for orders in relation to that had not materialised.

Behind the factory there was a sewage works with its own accompanying problems. In summer the smell was bad enough but the seasonal gathering of the bluebottle fraternity was something else. It had been observed that they usually took morning exercise by flying around in a huge swarm, circling around the source of the smell as if attempting to determine the exact point of maximum aroma. A sudden dive on an unsuspecting load of sewage by a million or so bluebottles may not be everybody's idea of a spectacle, and if you happened to be close by you would be well advised to get inside the nearest shelter as fast as you could. The cloud machine factory had had to take a number of measures to minimise the bluebottle impact. Factory windows were made non-opening and an air conditioning plant had been installed to make the environment as pleasant as possible, and each employee was given an air freshener on a weekly basis during the height of the purge period.

Cirrus and Puffy arrived at the factory and presented themselves at the reception desk. The sales manager, Mr Tideswell, welcomed them and exchanged a few pleasantries before taking them to the factory showroom. They were no strangers to the factory: they had been here many times before to get work done on the Nimbus. They walked along a corridor that led to the showroom and as they went through the entrance door they had to squint. There were no windows in the showroom since its contents were protected by secrecy, but everything was so pristine that everything reflected the powerful lighting embedded in the ceiling. Everything about the showroom was glossy. The walls, ceiling and floor shone, and there in the centre of this large room was the latest development in cloud machine technology the Star AW Mk1. Outwardly it looked just like the Nimbus, but the highly polished all white fuselage made it look superb.

"What does the AW stand for Mr Tideswell?" asked Cirrus.

"It's the latest All Weather machine."

Walking around the machine, Puffy spotted that the name Nimbus II had been painted on the nose. They must be confident of a sale he thought. There was no doubt that the machine looked good when it appeared on show like this.

"Although you can't tell just by looking, these fan duct motors are the very latest."

"I know, we have read all about them," said Cirrus.

"The entry to the machine has been kept just the same as before! If you wish to prevent anyone gaining access when you are not present you just press this button on the side and the entry ladders will retract and the entry door will close. No-one can reverse that process before keying in your code number using this keyboard."

He lifted a small panel on the side of the craft to reveal the keyboard.

"You can de-activate the keyboard by placing a key here and turning it like this."

Mr Tideswell demonstrated how it all worked, even though it was no different from the way it operated on their current machine.

They went on board the Star AW Mk1 to observe the internal features, but everything was much the same as before except that it had that smell of newness about it.

"You can't see the new communications and navigation equipment but it is installed and we have ensured that there is no change to the controls that you use to operate them. You will, however, note that there is a change on the flight engineer's control panel."

Puffy and Cirrus took a close look and could see the new addition to the machine's weather repertoire, 'snow and hailstones'. Both could be produced in varying degrees.

Snow could be light, heavy or sleet whereas hailstones could be large or small.

"You really can't see what this new model can do just looking around it so I'm going to show you a film that we have taken."

Mr Tideswell escorted the crew of the Nimbus to a room which had been set up as a small cinema and they sat down in plush seats to watch the weather show. It was all a bit strange, really, watching a cloud come flying by, to be told that that is the Star AW Mk1 and then watch it snowing. It looked good but it was still odd to watch.

There was then a short break before a second showing got underway. Another cloud came flying by and then hailstones started to drop from it, but it was hard to tell they were hailstones. The film then went to ground level, showing the hailstones impacting with the ground which was not altogether convincing, and Mr Tideswell could tell that from their faces.

"I think the best way for you to see what our new weather-maker can do is to have a demonstration flight."

Cirrus and Puffy jumped at the chance but they would have to wait until it was dark before they could do it.

As darkness began to fall, Cirrus and Puffy were introduced to the crew that would take them on the demonstration flight aboard the Star AW Mk1. Test pilot Johnny Black was the son of one of the Black brothers that founded the business and the test Engineer, Ronnie Blackemore, was the son of the co-founder. Introductions done, they all boarded the latest model and the crew set about getting organised. As the four fan duct motors were started, the lights in the showroom started to dim and doors at one end began opening to reveal the wharf outside. As the lights completely went out, the Star machine taxied out onto the wharf with the Manchester Ship Canal straight ahead. The machine momentarily stopped and then ascended into the darkness. The acceleration was considerably greater than Cirrus or Puffy had previously experienced and was a clear indication of the extra power available with the new motors. They rapidly reached five thousand feet and then headed west towards the Irish Sea.

Flying at fifty knots, Cirrus couldn't resist pointing out that this contravened the rules set out in the **Cloud Machine Rules of Operation Manual.** Test Pilot Johnny replied that this new machine was exempt from that rule. The limit had been raised to fifty knots. In double quick time they passed over Liverpool and came to a hover over the Irish Sea. Ronnie switched on the atomiser and they began to immerse themselves in cloud, a Cumberland Grey to be exact. They atomised four million gallons of the Irish Sea and it was quite a substantial cloud when they had finished. The co-ordinates for Helvellyn in the Lake District were punched into the Soakometer/navaid and the cloud began to make its own way there. They pushed on at fifty knots and with a tail wind of ten knots it seemed like no time at all before they reached their destination. Overtaking other clouds being propelled by the power of nature's wind was really exciting and gave a good idea of the speed they were doing.

Over Helvellyn they began to snow and all this was clearly visible on the pop-up TV screen on the flightdeck. Only half the cloud was used making snow and when it stopped the summit of this Lake District Mountain was capped in it. It looked spectacular and it most certainly would be to the locals when they woke up in the morning. It was the middle of summer when all was said and done!

Johnny punched a fresh set of co-ordinates into his navigation equipment and they set off for Morecambe Bay in the opposite direction to the natural clouds out journeying that night, but none of them complained. In no time they were over the bay and Ronnie arranged to finish off their cloud by converting it into large hailstones. It was not too obvious that they were hailstoning, but the ships transiting in and out of Heysham knew it was as the great lumps hit their superstructures, waking those crew members currently off duty and getting their heads down.

Having dispensed with a Cumberland Grey, the Star AW Mk1 made the flight back to Salford and the wharf outside the factory of Black, Black & Blackemores. They landed just outside the open doors of the secret showroom and taxied straight in and switched off the four fan duct motors. As the showroom doors closed the lights came on. As they all exited this brand new machine, Mr Tideswell was waiting for them and he could see from the smiles on the faces of Cirrus and Puffy that he had a potential sale on his hands.

Terms

"Now what did you think of that, Captain Cumulus?" asked Mr Tideswell.

"Very impressive! The rate of ascent to five thousand feet was spectacular and we flew everywhere much faster than we do at present."

"You could get more work done in a given time and the more efficient motors would allow you to do it much cheaper with lower running costs."

"You are probably right," replied Cirrus, thinking to himself that this was typical salesman talk.

"What did you think about the snow and hailstone feature?"

"The snow was very good. I could see the results on Helvellyn very well indeed. It's more difficult to assess the hailstone. I think we would need to be underneath one of your new machines when it was hailstoning to appreciate it."

At this point Mr Tideswell disappeared for a moment and then returned with a thin sheet of metal.

"This sheet of metal is the same thickness as that used in car production and we used it in a trial test to measure the effect of our hailstones. You can see the many points of impact."

If this had been my car, thought Cirrus, I would not be very pleased.

"These dents could only have been made by substantial hailstones falling at a high velocity," went on Mr Tideswell.

Once the virtues of the new model cloud machine had been highlighted, the conversation turned to the question of buying.

"How would you like to own one of our new Star AWMk1's, Captain?"

Cirrus looked at Puffy for support and a nod of the head from his colleague was enough to tell him to go ahead and make a deal.

"I would love to own one but it really depends on the asking price."

"You could have this technological wonder for £1,000,000."

The crew of the Nimbus were not surprised by this figure, they knew that the development costs would be steep and there was only a small sales market for them.

"What would you give me for my old machine?" asked Cirrus.

There was a very small market for second hand machines but they tended to hold their prices well.

"How old is the Nimbus?"

"I got her new from you in 2003 so that makes her just ten years old."

"And what have you got on her atomometer?"

This is a device rather like a tachometer but it records the number of clouds that a cloud machine has made by recording how many times the process of atomising has taken place. Water must be atomised before it can be made into a cloud by a cloud machine.

"Three thousand, six hundred and fifty."

"That's not bad!" Mr Tideswell then pulled a small book out of his pocket and consulted some of its pages before making an offer.

"I'll give you £500,000 for the Nimbus and that's a very good offer."

"I'll go away and think about it and let you know in a couple of days," replied Cirrus.

"Well don't take too long; I have several other interested parties."

That was more typical sales talk thought Cirrus as he departed the factory, but he was pretty keen to buy this latest model.

Back at Wythenshawe, the Superintendant broached the subject of a new machine.

"So what did you think about this new model by Black, Black & Blackemore's Cirrus?"

"Brilliant, Mr Spite. It has a lot of virtues. It would be a lot more economical to operate and being able to produce snow and hailstones makes it unique amongst cloud machines."

"Are you buying one then?"

"I'm still considering it. It's a big capital outlay. Even taking into consideration the part exchange of my current machine, I would have an outlay of £500,000."

"You're not short of a bob or two Cirrus."

Cirrus was relatively well off, with two houses, one in Slaidburn, one in Ballyhalbert in Northern Ireland and two cars. He lived fairly frugally and didn't take holidays. His spare time was spent in Ballyhalbert. The money he had in the bank was largely to keep his current machine operating and to replace it at intervals of time, but £500,000 would be taxing his resources.

"I don't want my reserve cash reduced by so much so I may have to consider buying on a hire purchase agreement."

"There are Government grants for this purpose Cirrus. You could probably get a grant for half the amount you need. I could do that for you if you wish?"

It was extremely generous of Wythenshawe's Superintendent to offer to do that, and Cirrus accepted most gratefully.

"Look at this flashy job!" remarked Wally Lenticular to a group of his cloud machine owner colleagues as they walked around Wythenshawe Weather Centre's latest addition. Of all the machines currently parked in the Centre's huge hangar, it was the Star AW Mk1 that stood out from all the others. The glossy white paintwork made all the difference and the high polish finish deterred everyone from touching.

"Whose is this then?" someone asked.

"Judging by the name on its nose, I would say it belongs to Cirrus Cumulus," remarked someone else.

Wally stepped up to the nose of the new craft and looked at the name, Nimbus II.

It could only belong to his pal Cirrus with a name like that.

"They say this new machine can make snow."

"An it can make hailstones."

"Blimey, that's versatility for you!"

"That's more like bad weather for you!"

The comments came thick and fast but there was no doubt that a degree of envy was on show. It was just a pity that Cirrus and his Flight Engineer were not there to hear it.

"I wonder who's going to get the first lot of snow from this machine?"

This question would be answered in the not too distant future.

# A NEW WEATHER MAKING RESEARCH CENTRE

Abigail calls

Cirrus was busy reading the instruction manual for his new cloud machine, Nimbus II, when Puffy burst in to the room both agitated and excited.

"Skipper, Abigail has just been on the phone and says she is calling to see you tomorrow. She says she will stop for tea but will have to leave afterwards."

"Well, that's good news Puffy."

"I'll organise a meal and get some flowers in."

"Don't bother with the flowers; you know how things can change. A good meal will do nicely."

Puffy withdrew from the lounge most pleased that Cirrus had not taken the huff with Abigail after his last disappointment.

It was a warm night in Slaidburn and, what with that and the nervousness he was experiencing, Cirrus couldn't get off to sleep and he tossed and turned for what seemed like an eternity. When morning finally arrived he took a shower and felt considerably refreshed. Puffy made him a grand breakfast to set him up for the day, but the side effect of that was that he started to think again about the implications of what he was about to do, but an idea started to gel with him. It would be premature to explore his new idea too soon; there was something else to do first.

The door bell rang and Puffy went to answer it. After a moment or two, the lounge door opened and in stepped a delightful looking Abigail. Her tall slim build went well with the plain pink dress she chose to wear and matching lipstick. Cirrus found it difficult to get his words out and before he did, it was Abigail who began speaking.

"Good morning Cirrus, it's so nice to see you. I want to apologise for the other week but I'm afraid it was due to the latest bit of work I have been doing. In fact that's the reason I must go after tea. The good news is, though, that I will have finished the job in a week's time."

"Oh forget that Abigail! I know the nature of weather-making; it's always an erratic business."

"What was it that was so important that you wanted to say to me?"

That was the 64,000 dollar question and it put him very much on the spot.

"You seem very nervous Cirrus. Is there something the matter?"

"No, no, there is nothing wrong. I went to Lancaster the other week to get you something." Cirrus fumbled with a small package and when he had finally got rid of the wrapping paper, it was clearly a ring box. Looking at Abigail, he gathered all his courage and more or less blurted it out: "Abigail, I would like you to become my wife."

She had guessed that he was intending to propose but it still seemed like a surprise when it happened. She could never imagine how Cirrus would propose to her.

The couple stood looking at each other, one waiting for an answer and the other trying to decide what to say.

"Abigail, I do love you!"

"Cirrus, I love you too but I must think about this."

Suddenly, Cirrus felt tremendously deflated and embarrassed. Had he misjudged things? Had he made a fool of himself? Suddenly he was starkly aware of the age gap between Abigail and himself.

Abigail could see that Cirrus was sinking into a state of despair and rapidly set about repairing the emotional damage.

"Cirrus I want you to know that I have come to love you most dearly and, so much so, that I want to be sure that if I become your wife, it's not going to change all those things so dear to you. I know that is probably not what you want to hear from me right now, but just give me a little time and I will give you my answer."

Cirrus reluctantly accepted her decision and something of a pregnant pause followed before any further conversation was embarked upon.

"What do you think about your new cloud machine Cirrus?"

The remaining part of Abigail's visit was a bit of a strain and both parties were somewhat relieved when it was time to for her to go. When she did go, it left Cirrus feeling downhearted and Puffy could detect that all had not gone to plan, but he didn't choose to ask anything at this time.

"Do you know Puffy White, that you are the reason that Abigail won't get engaged to Cirrus?" asked Carol in a forthright way.

"What do you mean? I haven't done anything!"

"That's it you great dope, you haven't done anything. Abigail is worried that if she marries Cirrus it'll split you and him up and you won't have anywhere to live."

Puffy had never really thought much about the situation but now that she had come to mention it, he could see her point of view.

"How did you get to know anyway?"

"Lucy, Abigail's sister, told me. She and Abigail are very close and they share each other's burdens."

I wish they would share mine, thought Puffy.

Another interesting proposal

It was that time of morning again and Cirrus was sitting comfortably in his lounge reading the Daily Gloom and drinking a cup of coffee. Puffy, on the other hand, was on standby for the latest outburst on how the Country should be sorted out. After a number of years experience, he had still not worked out the most satisfactory strategy for handling his skipper when he got into one of his 'I know what's best for the Country' tirades. For the moment it was a case of keeping stum and perhaps agreeing with the odd nod of the head before tactfully withdrawing.

Scanning through the various pages, Cirrus was drawn to an article in the centre spread of the paper which read –

Weather Expert Works on a Bright Future

Wondering what on earth that was all about, he read on to discover that the expert was Professor W. Flood, which was a slightly ironic name, he thought, from the University of Northern England. Professor Flood was the Head of the University Department of Weather Studies and had been studying weather for most of his life. He had written many books on the subject and was held in great esteem by scientists and meteorologists around the globe. His latest studies had led to his latest thesis, which was being seriously debated in the forum of weather experts.

The world's pattern of winds, rain, drought, floods, tornados etcetera are extremely difficult to predict, wrote the Professor, and on many occasions the Authorities were caught out and had to take emergency measures. Ruined crops, death and destruction often followed freak conditions that had not been foreseen. If all this weather could be brought under control, the world could be a better place, the Professor went on.

Cirrus couldn't agree more, but how did the Professor propose to harness the forces of nature? He continued reading and found that a case was being made to fund research into that very thing. It was being argued that there were two steps in the process, the first being to stop the existing winds from blowing and, the second to remove all the clouds in the atmosphere. In other words, ridding the earth of weather.

This sounds a bit like the mad idea Vannin in the Isle-of-Man had, thought Cirrus, but he was gripped by what he was reading and carried on to learn more about the Professor's theory.

The article went on to describe that it may be possible to make our own weather to order. It only takes wind and cloud to create weather and, if we made our own wind and cloud, we could make it go to wherever it was needed and when it was needed. This would bring order to our weather and enable the earth's resources to be far more efficient. Food production could be greatly improved and starvation eradicated. Weather-related disasters could become a thing of the past. In fact the more you think about it the more it had going for it, the professor argued.

Cirrus was stunned by the power of the Professor's argument. He was well aware that clouds could be made because that was the business he and his colleagues were in. He was also aware that winds could be man made; he remembered clearly the wind that had been generated by the wind farm off the coast of Cumbria that had propelled his search team to St.Kilda to rescue Lucy Windrush. This is not so far fetched, thought Cirrus, but were does Wythenshawe Weather Centre and The Guild of Cloud-Owners' fit into all this?

Professor Flood made out a very compelling case for the Government to fund a research establishment to work on his theories and the very idea was currently being debated and the outcome was eagerly awaited.

Cirrus was full of anticipation as a result of what he had read and made a point of mentally noting that he must keep an eye out to see how it developed. He didn't have long to wait. A couple of days later it was announced on TV that the Government had agreed to set aside funding for the establishment of a Weather Making Research Centre, the details of which would be made public in due course.

For the next few days, each time Puffy brought the Daily Gloom in for his skipper to read, he was greeted with enthusiasm,which baffled him. But he didn't mind if he wasn't going to be on the receiving end of any political outpourings. The anticipated information was not long in coming and again it was in the form of a centre spread.

Details of New Weather Making Research Centre Announced

Professor W.Flood has been charged with the responsibility of setting up a Weather Making Research Centre within the University of Northern England's Department of Weather. The new research establishment will be developed on the old Royal Aircraft Establishment airfield at Llanbedr on the Cardigan Bay coast of Wales.

The article went on to stress that the Centre will have formal links with Cloud Machine Manufacturer Black, Black & Blakemore's in deeper Salford along with Wythenshawe Weather Centre and, 'The Guild of Cloud-Owners'. The aim of the new Centre was stated as follows: 'The aim of the Research Centre is to make weather to order a worldwide practical possibility.'

The location was excellent, thought Cirrus. Llanbedr airfield is right by the sea and in a fairly isolated location which would keep things away from prying eyes. Little fuel would be expended by any cloud machines operating there since it was only a hop over the sand hills to Cardigan Bay, a source of water to atomise and make into a cloud. It also had suitable hangar space to house a number of machines. Cirrus would watch out to see how things evolved.

The First Faculty

Everybody associated with Wythenshawe Weather Centre was taking a keen interest in the establishment of the Weather Making Research Centre at Llanbedr and regular reports were being featured in 'The Guild of Cloud-Owners' monthly journal, The Monthly Downpour. The first report focused on the setting up of the first faculty which was to be called the Faculty of Cloud Making. Its first Head was Doctor John Grey but no-one at Wythenshawe had ever heard of him.

The Faculty of Cloud Making had already ordered a research machine from Black, Black & Blakemore's and it was one of the latest models, a Star AW Mk1, and would be officially named Northern Star 1 at some time in the future. The new Head of the Faculty, Dr Grey, had already announced his intention of working closely with Wythenshawe Weather Centre on cloud-making in the future.

Dr Grey had outlined the field of research his Faculty would be engaged in. To begin with, it would look at ways of improving the production of clouds currently being done by Wythenshawe's team. That meant they would be looking at Cumulus, which had been nicknamed Westmorland Whites in the past, Altocumulus, referred to as Cumberland Greys and, finally those famous Manchester Blacks, which in reality were Cumulonimbus clouds.

Improving existing clouds was only one side of the research coin. The Faculty also had plans to find a way to manufacture Cirrus, Stratus, Castellanus and Lenticularis.

Cirrus takes the form of delicate white filaments with a fibrous or silky appearance, whereas Stratus is usually a grey cloud layer with a uniform base. Castellanus, on the other hand, are heaped clouds sharing a common base and, Lenticularis are lens shaped clouds formed in waves.

There was a view in the Faculty that if nature was to be mimicked then it must be done comprehensively. The world was not to be denied what nature had nurtured over millions of years. The motto adapted by Dr Grey was, 'Nature by Replica'.

Further development

The next edition of the Monthly Downpour announced the creation of a second faculty at the new Weather Making Research Centre at Llanbedr. Things were progressing at a fast pace. The new Faculty was called The Faculty of Cloud Removal and Doctor Chris Blue was appointed as its Head. Like Dr Grey, no-one at Wythenshawe had ever heard of Dr Blue.

The Centre had placed an order with Black, Black & Blakemore's for a second machine, another Star AW Mk1, to be used by this latest Faculty and it was to be named Northern Star 2.

Salford's cloud manufacturer would be heavily involved in the Faculty's research and a consultant from the Isle-of-Man had been engaged to help, somebody by the name of Vannin.

The purpose of the Faculty was to establish a means by which all the world's clouds could be dispensed with. The initial method would use a condenser, something which Mr Vannin had experience of. A factor which would have special emphasis concerned the business of where to take all the condensed clouds and rain them away. It would have to be in a designated area of sea devoid of humanity to avoid displeasure. There was also the issue of rising sea levels. At any given time there was an enormous amount of sea in the sky in the form of clouds. If the sky was emptied of clouds and all the vapour returned to earth as water, it could create a dangerous increase in sea levels and that must be avoided. It would be important to calculate how much of the sea needs to be kept in cloud form at any given time to keep the sea levels constant. This had important implications for The Faculty of Cloud Making.

The motto adopted by this latest Faculty was, 'Clear Skies'.

"I didn't think I would ever hear the name Vannin again," said Cirrus?

"I wonder how the University got to know about him," replied Puffy.

Neither could fathom how Mr Vannin could have been recruited, considering his past record of whisky making, and assumed it may have been because of his work with condensers but that had come to nought. Cloud removal did however reveal how ruthless Mr Vannin could be and they doubted he could be an asset in the long term.

Over the next five months another five Faculties were established and this phenomenal rate of progress staggered those taking an interest in the new research establishment. Each one was reported in the Monthly Journal.

Doctor Rob Kiljoy had been appointed as the Head of the Faculty of Rain Making and his name, like the others, was a mystery to the relatively small circle in the business of weather-making and cloud machine manufacture. Dr Kiljoy would have his own cloud machine to play with, another Star AW Mk 1, to be named the Northern Star 3. The motto of this new Faculty was, 'We help things grow'.

The main purpose of the research would be to concentrate on improving the process of making slight, steady and heavy rain, all other kinds being regarded as unnecessary. Further to this, the functions of intermittent rain, drizzle and torrential rain were to be deleted from the existing repertoire of current cloud machines. The Faculty would work closely with Black, Black & Blakemore's and Wythenshawe Weather Centre on these matters.

The most unique role for this new Faculty would, however, be the creation of a rain calendar for each continent on the planet. The object of the calendar would be to highlight how much rain each continent requires and when. This would make the job of controlling the earth's weather much easier and certainly make it predictable. This was the key to the success of the whole project. It would be a great boon to society and industry to know exactly when and where it was going to rain and, if you could add to that how much rain you were going to get, then you had everything you could desire from a weather point of view. If it was possible to do all the raining at night then one would have the perfect weather scenario. This was challenging work but it would be most rewarding if successful.

Thunder and Lightning

Progress at the new Research Centre went ahead in a relentless fashion and the next Faculty to be created was the fourth, to be followed by three more by the year's end. The range of research seemed amazing to those with an interest, but it was still a mystery regarding the experts that the University was finding to appoint as Faculty Heads.

The fourth Faculty was called the Faculty of Thunder and Lightning and its Head was Doctor Donald Blunder, yet another mystery find. Dr

Blunder would, like the others, have his own machine to play with and it would be called Northern Star 4, another of the latest craft from Salford. The faculty motto was, 'By Flash and Bang', which was quite descriptive.

The Faculty had four purposes to investigate. First was to find a better way of making lightning in a cloud machine than using a Van de Graaf generator. This was a rather crude way of doing it, in this day and age and, on top of that, it was not easy to do without getting huge sparks of electricity jumping about inside the machine, frightening the crew in the process. This was a pretty specialised field and the Faculty would link up with the British Electricity Generating Authority in order to get results.

Second, was to find a better way of making thunder and here again this was another specialised field and a link-up with a company called All Round Sound Effects Incorporated had been made to facilitate research.

The last two purposes were more theoretical than the first two. There was a requirement to carry out research to try and establish the true role, if any, of thunder and lightning in the natural order of things. If there was no role then why not eliminate the phenomena? There was also a requirement to define how thunder and lightning can be used to entertain society.

"Do you think the University has heard of us doing thunder and lightning for entertainment purposes skipper?" asked Puffy.

"It's quite possible," said Cirrus who then continued, "The Great Cloud Parade was very special."

That brought back vivid memories to the crew of Nimbus II.

Snow and sleet

The Faculty of Snow and Sleet was the next to be established, with Doctor Bernard Chaos as its Head. The Faculty motto was, 'From the sky came little crystals'. Another craft from Salford would be at the disposal of Dr Chaos and it would be named Northern Star 5. Black, Black & Blakemore's were doing excellent business out of the new Weather Making Research Centre.

The Faculty's job was to try and improve the production of light and heavy snow using cloud machines, and to try and establish if there was any practical role in life for sleet. A second function of the faculty was to improve on the current method of producing large and small hailstones and once more to establish if there is any practical purpose that they fulfil.

Cirrus got to discuss the topic of the new Research Centre with Mr Spite. He was becoming a little concerned at the future for both himself and his fellow cloud machine owners, along with that of Wythenshawe Weather Centre. The way things appeared to be going there may not be a need for the kind of service they currently provided.

"I don't think you have much to worry about Cirrus. Frankly, I don't think there is any chance that anyone can control the world's weather."

"But they are spending huge amounts of money on the project."

"The Government throws money at all kinds of daft things. More than likely, someone in Government is going to make a fat fortune out of it all."

"Suppose they succeed?"

"In that case, all it means is that the work that comes in to Wythenshawe will largely be from a central source, and it makes little difference to you where it comes from, it's just a job. From my point of view, there is no reason why individuals shouldn't continue to order weather on a small scale, especially for entertainment, and it could make your life much easier if you had a regular pattern to your weather delivery work."

Cirrus had to agree with the latter point.

Dealing with wind

The last two Faculties to be established gained more interest from the members of the Guild of Cloud-Owners' than all the previous five. They both seemed to have a considerable degree of novelty value that appealed to their sense of fun but they also realised that there was a possible scientific benefit to them and they followed their development keenly.

A certain Doctor Bertram Nott was appointed Head of the Faculty of Wind and the name sounded familiar but no-one at Wythenshawe could put their finger on why. The Faculty would have its own machine which would be known as the Northern Star 6. The motto, 'Invisible Force', had been adopted to represent the force the Faculty was to concentrate its work on.

The Ministry of Wind Farms would work closely with the Faculty of Wind to pursue its aims. The first priority would be to develop methods of producing worldwide winds of varying direction and strength. The second was to develop methods of ensuring winds could blow at specific altitudes in the atmosphere.

The Faculty would also investigate the role of breezes, gusts, tornados and whirlwinds so that they could be eliminated if they were not serving any purpose other than to cause chaos.

Probably the greatest challenge was the one that it would work on in conjunction with the Faculty of Rain Making and that was to establish a wind calendar for each continent. This calendar would indicate when a wind was required to blow and where. Further details of a given wind would include its direction, strength, duration and altitude. It may even indicate the distance over which its influence would be felt.

The last Faculty

The last Faculty to be created at Llanbedr was very prominently announced in the Monthly Downpour. Over a period of seven months the Weather Making Research Centre had made a remarkable start. The real purpose of research had begun, but only on a limited basis, since the seven Star AW Mk1 cloud machines ordered from Black, Black & Blakemore's in deeper Salford would take some considerable time to manufacture. At least the staff and infrastructure was in place at Llanbedr to take advantage when the craft arrived.

The last Faculty to be established was the Faculty of Special Effects. This Faculty would conduct research into fog and mist and attempt to establish if nature used them for any special reason. The purpose of giving a cloud colour and making it glow would also be a focus for research along with its possible roles, including entertainment. The idea of using a Morse key to send messages using a glowing cloud would be fully explored. The recent experience of Wythenshawe's machine, Nimbus, guiding home a lost ship using this technique had had a strong influence on the inclusion of research into Morse clouds. Finally, research would take place on some more bizarre ideas, like creating pea soup fog and raining cats and dogs. The opportunity and need for this to be done are few and far between, but they had been asked for, and they had been done.

The motto adopted for this incredible Faculty was simply, 'We can do anything', and the new Head appointed was Doctor Whatsit but no-one had ever heard of him. He had, however, already announced his desire to work closely with the Cloud Machine Manufacturers in Salford and Wythenshawe Weather Centre. He acknowledged the work they had already done in this field.

Board of Directors

Soon an announcement appeared on the notice board at Wythenshawe telling everyone that the Superintendent, Mr Spite, had been appointed as one of the Board of Directors at the new Weather Making Research Centre. He would be joining Sheila Flood, the wife of Professor Flood who was the Head of the Centre. Sheila was also the daughter of one of the Black brothers that set up the cloud manufacturing business in Salford. Several MPs had also been appointed to the Board.

One question on everybody's lips was where did all the Head of Faculties come from and what did the members of the Board of Directors have to offer. They all had one thing in common and that was that none of them had ever been involved in cloud machines, with the exception of Sheila Flood and Mr Spite. A little bit of digging revealed that all the other Directors had involvement with Companies that stood to benefit from the money spent by the new Research Centre. Not much difference there then, thought many of the cloud machine crews.

"Is Mr Spite leaving Wythenshawe to take up his new position?"

"Who's going to take his place?"

"He's not leaving; it's a part time job on the Board of Directors," replied Mr Spite's secretary, Goldilocks.

"Well that's a relief because he would take some replacing."

"Hear, hear!"

The future would be the judge of the wisdom of setting up the Research Centre in the Department of Weather in the University of Northern England. For the moment it was weather as usual and time to get on with any work that was available. Most cloud machine owners were busy looking at the work board in Wythenshawe to see where their next remuneration would be coming from, rain or no rain!

PUT A DENT IN IT

Browsing

Cirrus had popped down to the Weather Centre in Wythenshawe to take a look at the 'jobs available' board. Since buying the latest model of cloud machine from Black, Black & Blackmore's, there was a need to keep earning. The current cost of fuel, not to mention maintenance costs, was pretty high these days and it all added to the necessity of earning money.

Browsing the jobs available board, a job delivering large hailstones caught his eye and he took the information card down to take a closer look. The information was fairly brief and simply gave a latitude and longitude at which large hailstones were to be deposited in the dark.

"That's rather weird," thought Cirrus.

The only other information shown was the approximate dates when the job must be done. There was nothing to indicate who the job was being done for.

Thinking to himself that the Nimbus II was the only cloud machine available that could deliver large, or small, hailstones, Cirrus decided to take the card along to Mr Spite's office and see if he could get any more details.

"Good morning Cirrus, what can I do for you?"

"I've taken this card off the jobs available board. I think I am the only person able to do the job, but the card doesn't give much information."

"It tells you when it must be done, where it must be done, and what must be done. What more do you want?"

"Well, for a start, who is the job for, and how much are they paying?"

"Ah! All I can tell you is that the Company that wants the job done is a very reputable European Company but it wishes to remain anonymous. As far as the fee is concerned, the Company knows that this is a specialised job and they will be paying a fee that amply reflects that. Off hand, I can't remember how much, but I can tell you it would be very much worth your while."

Cirrus felt a bit uncomfortable with the fact that the Company wished to remain anonymous. He asked himself if it could be a dodgy job. On the other hand, it was unlikely that a reputable European Company would be promoting something illegal or questionable.

Mr Spite became aware of the anxiety on the face of Cirrus and stepped in to reassure him.

"I don't think you have anything to worry about Cirrus. It's not our job to determine what should, or what should not, be done. That is the responsibility of the company asking for the job to be done."

"Are you suggesting that if we were asked to break into a bank, we should just do it?"

Mr Spite coughed and spluttered before regaining his composure.

"Look Cirrus, I think you will be fine taking this job on, and you will be guaranteed a good fee."

After taking a few moments to think about it, Cirrus decided he would do it.

He was moved by the fact that it was a reputable European Company that he would be working for and that sealed the deal for him, but he still felt a degree of suspicion.

A big surprise

All was quiet in the Slaidburn home of the Nimbus crew. For once, Cirrus was on his own. Puffy had gone away for a few days on family business, or so he said. The upshot of this was that Cirrus was left to fend for himself. It was not a big problem; it just meant that in the absence of Puffy, meals would become a bit more basic and he would have to go into the village himself for a copy of the Daily Gloom.

Breakfast consisted of three slices of double-sided, black toast and a cup of tea. A 'boil in the bag' meal of kippers would suffice for an evening meal and several ready- made meals in the deep freeze, that could be put in the microwave were all that was required until Puffy got back. Coping with Puffy not being at home was no big issue but the evenings were long without any company and generally, the house had a feeling of emptiness about it.

Not long after breakfast, Cirrus nipped out to the village shop and on his return he went into the kitchen to make a coffee. He heard a car come into the drive, followed by the closing of two doors.

"I wonder who that can be?" he thought.

There was a knock on the front door and he walked down the hall to answer it. When Cirrus opened the door he had the biggest shock of his life. Standing on the front step was Puffy in a splendid dark suit with a white rose in his left lapel, and a charmingly dressed Carol Aspinall, also with a white rose attached to her dress. Each of them had a cheek to cheek smile.

"Hello skipper, meet Mrs White."

For a moment, Cirrus was taken aback. Could it be true? It must be, they were standing in front of him.

Before he could say anything, Carol flung her arms around him and kissed him, leaving behind evidence of her ruby red lips.

"You are both married then?" enquired Cirrus.

"Just this very morning skipper and what a bargain I got."

"Don't you go calling me a bargain, like something you bought in a shop, Mr White!"

"Come on inside and tell me all about it".

Carol dashed off to the kitchen to make everyone a drink whilst Cirrus and his faithful engineer, Puffy, went ahead into the lounge.

"You kept that secret Puffy. I had no idea you two were going to get spliced."

"We had been building up to it skipper, but suddenly we made a decision. You know what it's like in our line of business. You don't know what's happening from one week to the next. One week it's rain we are delivering, one week it's a pretty cloud, another week it's a thunderstorm, and Carol being in the same business, well our clouds are always passing each other in the night sky, and we only get to meet now and again so we both decided to make the best of it."

Where did you get married?"

"We called in the Registrar's Office in Clitheroe, and they just had a spare slot, so we thought, well, why not?"

"Who did you get to witness the marriage?"

Carol came back into the room at this point.

"We went outside and saw this old couple who looked ever so pleasant, and we asked them," Carol replied.

"They were ever so nice about it," said Puffy.

The conversation moved on to practical matters.

"How are you both planning to earn a living?"

"Nothing is going to change. Puffy will continue working for you on the Nimbus, and I will continue as the engineer for Albertino, on board the Astro. We both realise that our work will only allow us to be together on odd occasions but we have both agreed that that is how we like it."

Well I'm glad they are agreed on that, thought Cirrus.

"Where are you both going to live?" asked Cirrus, dreading the probable answer as he did so.

"We had a stroke of luck there skipper."

Hell, thought Cirrus.

"In Church Street, here in the village, and only a few yards from the entrance to the Aurora Cloudealis, a little cottage came free for renting and we got it."

"That was good luck."

"But most of the time skipper, I will be living with you as usual. There's no point in living alone when Carol's not here."

That was a great relief to Cirrus who was beginning to panic that his world was suddenly being turned upside down.

"That's very good to know Puffy."

"We both thought you would like to know that Captain," said Carol.

"Carol, I think that from now on you should call me Cirrus. We are, almost, family now."

Carol moved across to Cirrus and gave him a kiss for being so understanding and warm towards them both, and it left him with a left cheek that now matched his right but she didn't let on.

Cirrus got up and disappeared for a moment and when he returned he had a jug in his hand marked 'Rob's tea'. Puffy had never discovered the significance of the marking on the jug, but he did know that it only made an appearance on very special occasions. A strong smelling fluid was poured from the jug into three glasses which they all raised in their outstretched hands to make a toast.

"To the happy couple!"

"To us!"

Having taken a drink, Carol coughed out loud as it cascaded down her throat.

"Heavens! What is that?"

"That my dear, is Rob's tea!"

"Some tea," she replied.

The three of them spent a pleasant afternoon in the Cumulus home, but eventually the time came for Carol and Puffy to leave and head for their Church Street cottage. As they got up to leave Cirrus gave them an envelope.

"That's my wedding present to the pair of you but don't open it until you get to your place."

"That's very kind of you Cirrus."

"Thanks skipper."

"And don't forget Puffy, we do have a job to do, delivering hailstones."

"Any idea when we will do it skipper?"

"Oh, it will keep for a couple of days."

The newly-married couple stepped outside the front door and, bidding Cirrus goodbye, they started walking down the drive whilst Cirrus watched on.

When they reached the gateway they looked back and waved before disappearing into Church Street.

This was, felt Cirrus, a real turning point in his life. Time marches on and nothing stands still. With a forlorn feeling, he stepped back inside the house and as he did so he couldn't help laughing.

That cheeky bugger Puffy White had gone and got hitched to a lovely young woman almost half is age. How the bloody hell had he done it?

Another dram was poured from that special jug and the world temporarily became a better place.

Back to making weather

Cirrus missed having Puffy for company, especially in the evenings but soon it was time to deliver hailstones. Puffy called round at Aurora Cloudealis every morning and hence, it was not difficult for Cirrus to collar him.

"Puffy, we better get on with delivering those hailstones. We have a window of time in which to do it, and the window is going to end soon."

"Ok skipper, when are we off?"

"I think we need to get away tomorrow."

"No problem skipper, the rest will do me good."

Cirrus did not pursue why Puffy may be in need of a rest; he could probably guess.

Early the next morning, Cirrus and his faithful engineer were on their way to Wythenshawe Weather Centre by car and to begin with there was little conversation. Cirrus didn't want any details about the virtues of married life and Puffy, evidently, just wanted to catch up on lost sleep.

On arrival at Wythenshawe, the crew of Nimbus II reported to the Centre's office before making their way into the huge hangar. Their new cloud machine certainly stood out from all the rest with its shiny new paintwork.

Puffy lifted a small panel on the side of the fuselage and pressed a button. The entry ladders started to emerge from under the entry door and, when fully extended, reached the ground. At the same time, the entry door opened outwards. The crew embarked and before making their way to the cockpit, Puffy pressed a button to retract the entry ladders and close the door.

Once inside the cockpit, Cirrus sat in the pilot's comfortable leather seat and picked up his checklist of cockpit drills before starting and checking the four fan duct motors. Whilst this was going on, Puffy stowed the rations that they always took on board before doing a job and then sat himself down at the Flight Engineer's station. He switched on the radio and made contact with Wythenshawe Control.

Being late in the evening, it was dark outside and, therefore, safe to get airborne. There were strict rules banning cloud machines from being observed by the general public, unless there were extenuating circumstances. Cirrus gave Puffy the nod that the four motors were all functioning as they should and he was ready to move. Puffy asked for permission to taxi and when clearance was given the Nimbus II moved forward in the hangar before turning toward the main doors. As the cloud machine moved, the hangar lights started to dim and the great doors started to open. The lights had fully extinguished by the time the doors had fully opened and the Nimbus emerged into the darkness outside. A number of cloud machine colleagues had gathered to witness the start of the maiden flight or at least the start of its maiden job.

The Nimbus came to a stop on the apron just outside the hangar and Cirrus ran up the motors. When he was satisfied that they were delivering the right amount of thrust, he signalled to Puffy to get take off clearance. This was essential to avoid any potential collision with either incoming or outgoing aircraft from nearby Manchester Airport. With clearance given, Cirrus pulled back the control column which altered the angle at which the motors were pointing and when they came to the vertical, the Nimbus shot into the sky. It took the breath away from the crew not to mention the spectators and they were approaching five thousand feet with considerable velocity. Cirrus had to ease the control column forward gently to slow down the rate of ascent and it took some fine judgement to gently level out at exactly five thousand feet.

"Phew, that was scary. I'm going to have to practise that a few times. We nearly overshot our hover height."

"I nearly overshot too, skipper!"

After spending a moment hovering and getting clearance to move out of the Machester Control Zone, Cirrus switched on his Identification Beacon which would tell all the ground controllers of the various air traffic radars exactly who he was and at what height he was. They could follow his course on their radar screens. With that job done, the Nimbus headed out on a westerly course to reach the Irish Sea. Using the same throttle settings as he did on his old machine, Cirrus could see that they were travelling much faster than they would have done previously, and the journey to the spot at which they usually came to a hover before atomising water was reached in a much shorter time. The more powerful motors were making everything happen much faster.

Coming to a hover, Cirrus gave the order to atomise 4,000,000 gallons of the Irish Sea and make a Manchester Black. This was the most ferocious looking cloud that they could make. Not all the water that was atomised took on the form of cloud vapour, some was stored in the saddle tanks mounted on the side of the Nimbus and some was stored as ice in the refrigerators. Whilst all this was happening, Cirrus punched the latitude and longitude of his destination into his Soakometer/navaid, ready for the journey to Upper Heyford in Oxfordshire. Within thirty minutes the Nimbus was in the centre of its own huge black, menacing cloud and it left its location over the Irish Sea for its destination. It was, perhaps, fortunate that its flight would go unobserved in the night for it was not a pleasant thing to look at.

Cirrus followed the progress of the Nimbus on his Plan Position Indicator and Puffy also kept an eye on their track using a chart which he had spread out on his chart table. He kept glancing at the PPI and then placing a mark on his chart. Using a chart was helpful since it covered the whole of the UK, whilst the PPI only gave an image with a twenty-five mile radius either side of the Nimbus. The pop-up tv screen on the flight deck also helped, by providing a view of where they were heading, care of the infra-red equipped tv camera mounted on the top of the machine.

Navigating to their destination in the dark was no problem for the crew of the Nimbus and they arrived in a matter of hours, much faster than they would have done previously. Nimbus automatically came to a hover over Upper Heyford and Cirrus decided to take a look at the place that was going to be on the receiving end of his large hailstones before depositing them. To do that he had to perform a large circuit around his target to allow the TV camera, which was mounted on the top of the machine, to have a chance of seeing the target. From the view he obtained, and which he confirmed using the chart Puffy had on his table, he could see that the target below them was the old American Air Force Base.

Having observed his target, Cirrus brought the Nimbus to the hover again in its bombing position and then descended, with great care, to two thousand feet before giving the order to Puffy to make large hailstones and drop them. The way this was actually done was pretty ingenious. The ice in the refrigerators was automatically broken up and shot out from exit holes fitted around the craft's fuselage. At the same time, this ice was replaced by freezing the water stored in the saddle tanks and when that was exhausted, then the vapour of the outside cloud was sucked back aboard through vacuum suction holes around the craft, condensed back into water and then frozen before being broken up and spit out as hailstones. A truly fantastic process and it worked!

There was no way of telling what impact the hailstoning was having down below but, up above, the Manchester Black was rapidly shrinking and when it was approximately a quarter of its original size Cirrus gave the order to stop. It was important to preserve some cloud for the journey home.

With the hailstoning finished, Cirrus punched the co-ordinates of a position over the Irish Sea near Liverpool into his Soakometer/navaid and off the Nimbus went on its homeward flight. They arrived at their destination after dawn had broken and consequently had a long wait until the following evening before they could rain themselves free from their present load of mist. Once they were free of the remnants of their Manchester Black, the crew got underway in the dark to Wythenshawe.

The arrival of the Nimbus from its maiden job was eagerly awaited by a crowd of well- wishing colleagues but it nearly ended in a catastrophe. Making the descent from five thousand feet to the apron outside Wythenshawe's huge hangar was a tricky thing to judge and Cirrus had a major struggle to stop the craft reaching mother earth at too great a velocity. It was a heavy landing to say the least and the Nimbus bounced back up into the air after its initial impact, but fortunately its second contact with terra firma was of a more permanent nature.

Once on the ground there was a loud cheer from the crowd accompanied by several streams of sweat running down the side of the face of its pilot. In no time the Nimbus was parked up inside the hangar and the crew were coming down the exit ladders to be greeted with a barrage of questions.

"How did the hailstones go?"

"It all went fine, no trouble at all."

There would be no chance of getting away to Slaidburn this evening with all the excitement about, and everyone headed off to The Silver Lining which was Wythenshawe's social club.

That was one of the great things about this weather work; there was never a dull moment, well at least not up there in the blue sky.

Repercussions

Without Puffy, Cirrus had to go out and get his own copy of the Daily Gloom and in doing so had the frustrating job of walking straight past the cottage his Flight Engineer was renting. He didn't think it was right to knock on the door and pop in for a coffee since Puffy was only recently married, and probably would not appreciate an early morning caller. There was nothing for it but to call in the village shop and then retire to his own place.

The Daily Gloom was up to its usual standard, with reports on everything that is wrong with the world and a lot of boring trivia. Still, it was something to pass the time with whilst having a coffee and Cirrus continued reading until he came to page four.

Over a thousand new cars damaged by freak storm.

Cirrus couldn't help feeling a sudden pang of anxiety. He had to continue reading the report.

In the early hours of Tuesday morning, over one thousand brand new, imported vehicles were badly damaged by a freak storm. The vehicles, in open storage on Upper Heyford Airfield in Oxfordshire, were all left badly dented after a severe fall of enormous hailstones. The vehicles were waiting to be distributed around the country to dealers to fulfil orders they had received. The manufacturer states that it could be months before they could deliver replacement vehicles and they were worried that they would experience a loss of business.

The report went on:

The Met Office state that they had no advance warning of any impending bad weather and had fully expected a relatively clear sky in the area at the time the storm occurred.

Cirrus couldn't help thinking that he could possibly have been involved in a case of industrial sabotage and he was worried. The question was, what should he do in these circumstances? There was only one thing for it; he would give the Superintendant at Wythenshawe a call and arrange a face to face meeting.

"Look Cirrus, you are taking all this far too seriously. All you did was hailstone and a few vehicles got dented. It happens!"

"A few vehicles Mr Spite! There were over a thousand and the manufacturer says it will take months to replace them. They are expecting to lose a lot of business and it's all down to me. I think you have duped me; I think this was a case of industrial sabotage."

"You did a legitimate job for a reputable company Cirrus, and that's all there is to it."

"Don't give me that. If any investigation takes place, the Police may well ask if any cloud machines could have been involved, and when they find out that only my machine can deliver hailstones, it's me that will be for it."

"Alright Cirrus, alright! I admit that it is a European car manufacturer that is paying for the job, and a good fee they are paying too, and they do stand to benefit from the misfortunes of others, but there is no way anyone is going to put this damage down to anything other than nature and you can't sue nature. My advice to you Cirrus is to go home and put it all behind you. Nothing is going to come of it."

A couple of weeks passed by and Cirrus had heard nothing about the dents his hailstones had imparted on over a thousand vehicles at Upper Heyford. He had been lying low, hoping that nothing would come of his involvement with industrial sabotage, but it still nagged away at him.

It was good to have Puffy around again. Carol was away doing a job. Hopefully, not one involving industrial sabotage! Puffy brought a coffee into the lounge and a letter that had just arrived. Cirrus opened the letter to find a cheque for a very substantial sum of money. The sender was some kind of an agent working on behalf of an anonymous European Company. This made everything even more sinister than it was before. Cirrus was beginning to think that his hailstones were more of a liability than an asset and wished he'd never dropped them. He felt reluctant to take the money and decided not to deposit the cheque in his account for the time being.

Word gets out

"Captain, there's a call for you."

"Who is it Puffy?"

"It's Wally Lenticular. He wants a word with you."

"Ok. Put him on."

"Is that you Cirrus?"

"Hello Wally, its Cirrus here. What do you want to talk to me about?"

"Was it you that dropped that load of hailstones on Upper Heyford?"

"Why are you asking?"

"Well, I don't know if you have heard or not, but word is out that it was an act of industrial sabotage."

"Who says it is?"

"Some bloke that works for a big European vehicle manufacturer has turned 'whistle- blower'. It's in this morning's paper."

For once, Cirrus had not seen today's paper and was caught unawares by Wally.

"Are there any details about what was done?"

"Not really. No respectable paper is going to make a serious claim that hailstones have been deliberately dropped. They would be a laughing stock."

Cirrus couldn't help thinking that this was bound to happen. It was a serious mistake to have taken this job on.

"Does it say what's going to happen?"

"Apparently the Board of Trade is going to investigate. Was it you Cirrus?"

"I can't answer that Wally and I'm going to have to go now."

When Puffy came into the lounge he could see that something had not pleased his captain but was reluctant to ask what it was."

"Word has got out that that job I did was industrial sabotage."

"Do they know it was you skipper?"

"I don't know, but the Board of Trade is investigating."

"Don't worry skipper, you just did a legitimate job. You were not to know it was dodgy."

"I should have been more careful. I wondered why I was being paid such a lot of money to do that job. In fact, when you think about it, why would anyone want me to deliver hailstones? I can't think of any good reasons for hailstones. I wish I hadn't bought a machine that can produce them, and owning the only machine that currently has that ability is going to make it easy for the Board to track me down."

"Have a cup of coffee skipper and try and look on the bright side."

"There is one thing you can do for me Puffy."

"Just name it skipper."

Cirrus fumbled around to find the letter he had recently received and when he found it, he took out the cheque.

"I want you to arrange for this to be donated to 'The Head in the Sky' rest home."

"Are you not being a bit hasty skipper?"

Cirrus didn't answer. He left the lounge and headed for his study. He needed to think seriously about the latest development.

A week later a report appeared in the Daily Gloom regarding the investigation conducted by the Board of Trade into possible industrial sabotage and Cirrus studied its content intently. The Board had indeed found the case proved. A large European vehicle manufacturer had been found guilty and faced a huge compensatory fine which would go some way towards compensating the injured party. Cirrus read on to try and discover whether he had been implicated.

There was no reference within the report to Cirrus or his machine, the Nimbus, but Wythenshawe Weather Centre came out of it in a bad light. The Centre came in for a fair amount of criticism and a recommendation was made that it should put into place more vigorous job-vetting procedures. Whilst Cirrus was somewhat relieved that there was no reference to himself or his machine, he still felt apprehensive. He would have to face the Superintendant at Wythenshawe sooner or later and was unsure about the welcome he would receive, but it could have been a lot worse.

Facing Mr Spite

Puffy popped into the Aurora Cloudealis lounge to interrupt his captain's morning by announcing that he had received a message from Wythenshawe.

"What is it then Puffy?" asked Cirrus in a gloomy mood.

"You have to report to Mr Spite on Wednesday morning, at 10-00am sharp skipper."

"Damn!" This is what he had predicted would eventually happen.

Arriving at Wythenshawe Weather Centre, Cirrus went into the office of the Superintendant's secretary.

"Good morning Captain Cumulus. Mr Spite is expecting you."

"What kind of a mood is he in Goldilocks?"

Before Mr Spite's secretary could answer, his voice could be heard booming out.

"Miss Black, if Captain Cumulus has arrived, send him in right away!"

Goldilocks looked at Cirrus nervously and escorted him to Mr Spite's office. She knocked on his door and hearing the command, 'Come in,' she opened the door and signalled to Cirrus to go in and as he did so she whispered, "Good luck."

"Sit down Cirrus and have a drink."

That was not the reception that Cirrus had expected and he waited for the next move.

"I'm sure you are aware of the findings of the Board of Trade?"

"Yes, I am."

"It's all a load of tripe really. We are always doing questionable things and on many occasions for the Government. They have to put reports out like the one you read, just to cover themselves."

"You don't seem very concerned Mr Spite."

Cirrus, it goes on all the time, you just have to take it all with a pinch of salt."

"Are you not going to give me a dressing down?"

"Not at all Cirrus, but for official purposes, if asked, you are to say that you have been cautioned. By the way, have you been paid yet?"

"Yes, but I donated it to 'The Head in the Sky' rest home."

Mr Spite opened a drawer in his desk and pulled out a cheque. He handed it to Cirrus and said, "Was it this one?"

Cirrus recognised it immediately.

"This is the one. How did you get it?"

"Never mind that, just put it into your bank account when you get back. Don't forget, you just bought a new cloud machine."

"Miss Black, bring in my best malt whisky!"

NEW CREWS

An important advert

Oscar Blowhard studied meteorology at Hull University before getting a job with the Met Office in Exeter. His work had taken him around the country, and a good deal of his time had been spent on a variety of RAF stations which had resulted in his current interest in all things flying. He ended his time at RAF Valley and it was during this posting that he got to know about a course for cloud machine pilots.

The Guild of Cloud-Owners' was attempting to recruit a small number of new pilots to continue its important work based at Wythenshawe Weather Centre. A fair number of its current pilots were coming up to retirement age and replacements were going to be needed. The Guild planned to train its new pilots at its training centre at Bishops Court in Northern Ireland. Those that gained their Cloud Wings would be teamed up with experienced flight engineers, using existing machines at Wythenshawe.

Like all new pilots, they would be restricted in terms of what they could do until they gained proficiency, and their respective flight engineers would be the judge of that. Atomising water and creating a cloud was, of course, the first priority and linked to that was raining, initially just to get rid of the cloud. Even cloud manufacture was done on a kind of sliding scale, with Westmorland Whites first on the list and Manchester Blacks the last. Successful cloud makers would then progress on to making rain, again on a sliding list starting with drizzle and working through to a torrential downpour. The many other things that cloud machines do would feature later in their cloud-flying careers.

The induction process for any new cloud machine pilot could take several years, and like all the other pilots, they would keep a record of everything they did in a Cloud Pilot's Log Book which would be checked annually by the Superintendant at Wythenshawe. There was a rigorous regime in place to ensure that everyone involved in weather-making and delivery was up to the job.

There was no expectation for a new pilot to purchase his or her own cloud machine. By teaming up a new pilot with an experienced flight engineer they would also be teaming up with that flight engineer's craft. This was only possible by virtue of the fact that it is was a tradition for retiring pilots, who in ninety-nine per-cent of cases owned the machines, to pass them on to their flight engineers. Every machine was however, licensed in the skipper's name and this did create something of a legal challenge which the Guild's solicitors had spent a lot of time working on, but that was all resolved now.

The courses for cloud machine pilots at Bishops Court were very expensive to conduct and applicants would require a hefty sum of money in order to be eligible to undertake one. The Guild did, however, offer loans at extremely low rates. That was considered essential in order to attract the best potential recruits to the weather- making business.

Currently at Wythenshawe there were two flight engineers minus pilots and they and their machines were having a long term respite from weather pursuits and both were getting rather bored with all the enforced idleness. There is only so much that you can do with a cloud machine on the ground in a hangar and none of it concerned making or delivering weather.

Flight Engineer Henry Black was the proud current owner of the Greystuff which his pilot, the late Al Blighty, had left him in his will. Henry was desperate to get back to earning some money and although he was a little concerned about teaming up with a fledgling cloud machine pilot, he was still prepared to give it a go.

The circumstances surrounding Flight Engineer Larry Oliver were somewhat different. Larry's skipper, Arthur Treadmill, was serving a six month suspension. Whilst that had been the initial reason for Larry's grounding, the situation had changed. His pilot, Arthur, had met an Australian girl from Melbourne who had a share in a Boomerang factory and, since his wife Lily had ditched him, he decided that emigrating would, under the circumstances, not be a bad idea. With Arthur being the owner of the cloud machine, Drip, it left his flight engineer Larry in a difficult situation and a legal battle had ensued which found in Larry's favour and ownership was passed to him. What Larry needed now was for a pilot to be passed on to him and, under the circumstances, he was not overly fussy as to where he or she came from.

With two flight engineers, each with their own cloud machines, Wythenshawe Weather Centre was anxious to get recruiting. The Superintendant, Mr Spite, racked his brain to determine how he could encourage applicants for the course planned at Bishops Court Training Centre. He had been swayed by the notion that it may be advantageous to recruit potential trainees with a meteorological background. Although that made sense to a point, that was no guarantee that they would make good pilots but he was willing to try it. He had been helped in reaching this decision by the newly created Weather Making Research Centre at Llanbedr. The new centre had a need for seven pilots to fly their research machines and consequently was putting considerable funds into the course for pilots.

Discussions with Professor Flood at Llanbedr lead to the creation of an advertisement that would go to the Meteorological Office in Exeter which, in turn, would distribute it to the many locations that its Officers served in, around the country.

It was this very advertisement that attracted Oscar Blowhard into applying. Anything would be better than watching all the jet jockeys at Valley enjoying themselves whilst he was permanently land-based. What made the prospects look particularly good was the fact that on completion of the course there would be the chance of a job, with vacancies at both Llanbedr and Wythenshawe. Money was not an enormous problem either. Oscar had a few bob put to one side and the Meteorological Office were offering bursaries to successful applicants. When the course was completed, any new cloud machine pilots taking up a post at the Weather Making Research Centre would have any outstanding course fees paid. That was the thing that clinched it for Oscar and he requested an application form

You too could make rain whilst the going is good !

Fancy a career with a difference?

How about an office in a cloud?

Vacancies exist for trainee cloud machine pilots on course

CCMO/15/13

At Bishops Court Training Centre

A Guild of Cloud Machine Owners training establishment

Nine pilots' jobs up for grabs on completion

MET Office bursaries available

Loans available from the Guild at cheap rates

Interested?

Contact Wythenshawe Weather Centre for an application form

When Bertram Gust saw the advertisement for trainee cloud machine pilots he saw it more as a possible salvation than a career change. Bertram had a similar background to Oscar in so far as he had studied meteorology and ended up working for the Meteorological Office in Exeter. Bertram had gained his degree at Glasgow and, like Oscar, had been posted around the country to different airfields before arriving at his present post at Inverness.

Inverness was where Bertram had struck up a relationship with his wife who was the daughter of Angus and Mary MacCloud. Morag was a lovely young woman who had swept Bertram off his feet and, after a short courtship, the two of them married. It would have been better if the couple had waited before getting married and used the time to save. As it was, their shortage of funds forced them into accepting her parents' invitation to live with them for the time being.

Whilst Morag's parents were generous in offering them temporary accommodation they were most overpowering, and Bertram felt that he had lost something very dear to him, namely, his independence to make decisions. He frequently got frustrated with Morag's mother who always seemed to know what's best. The fact the she was often right was difficult to swallow, and he made several bad decisions just to be different.

Angus MacCloud was very proud of his Scottish culture and more often than not, was to be seen around the home wearing a kilt. That was in no way objectionable. Bertram admired his father-in-law's pride but he was less understanding when it came to listening to his bagpipe playing. Listening to bagpipes being played was fine in moderation, but in the case of Angus, who worked for a bagpipe manufacturer, and who was a champion of the Highlands, it was another matter. The frequency and duration of the home rehearsals was beginning to drive Bertram mad and the lack of understanding from either his mother-in-law or his wife, Morag, was severely impairing his desire to remain anywhere near Inverness.

The bottle of malt whisky on the shelf of the MacCloud home was ultimately to prove the downfall of Bertram. The golden nectar that he poured down his throat didn't get rid of the shrill of the pipes but it did give him an alcoholic sanctuary from which it was getting more and more difficult to recover. With a general lack of understanding and sympathy, the drinking became steadily worse and things came to a head when one day at work he forecast a day of fog or mist which resulted in the cancellation of a day's flights. Under normal circumstances that would have been the right thing to do, but when the fog or mist never materialised there were questions to ask and the smell of whisky on his breath provided an important answer.

A temporary suspension brought Bertram back to his senses and he knew that he had to get away from the MacCloud family home, but doing so was not going to be easy. Morag had refused to discuss the issue and when she informed her parents, they sided with her. There was no way of getting away from the fact that his marriage was coming to a premature Scottish Highlands end but the consolation was that so was the sound of the bagpipes.

Trainee cloud machine pilot, with a possible job at the end; that sounded pretty good to Bertram. He felt that he had already had his head in the sky for some time but it had all been a blur. If he completed this course and got a new job as a cloud machine pilot, he could perhaps get up there with the best, and it would all be in focus. Let's have a bash, he thought. And he requested an application form.

Over two hundred applications arrived at Wythenshawe to take up the places on the course at Bishops Court and they were all carefully sifted through. The process was lengthy but at the end twenty candidates were selected for interview and a date was set on which to conduct them. The interview board could offer places to ten candidates and hopefully the first round of interviews would see them selected. Both Henry Black and Larry Oliver certainly hoped that this would be the start of the solution to their current problems and could dream about their cloud machines getting back in business. Bertram Gust and Oscar Blowhard were amongst the applicants selected for interview.

At RAF Valley, Oscar got a load of banter from his Met colleagues but that was something he could cope with. What he needed to do now was to try and prepare himself for the forthcoming challenge. His knowledge of weather was extensive and because of where he was he also knew a fair amount about flying. But when it came to cloud machines and their operation, well, that was another matter. Bertram suffered a different kind of response from his colleagues; they were more than pleased that he had made a move to leave Inverness and its weather to them. Looking through a whisky laden pair of eyes had not been the most successful way of doing things. Like Oscar, Bertram had some homework to do to prepare himself for his forthcoming interview and it all had to be done in secrecy, for he had not told either Morag or the MacCloud family of his intentions.

Each of the interviews followed the same pattern and each candidate was rigorously tested on what they knew about meteorology and flying before moving on to what they knew about weather-making and delivery. The interviews were wound up by asking each candidate how much they knew about the new Weather Making Research Centre at Llanbedr as well as Wythenshawe Weather Centre. The latter would establish whether the candidate had taken the trouble to find out about these potential places of employment.

Both Henry Black and Larry Oliver sat in on the interviews. Ultimately, their new skippers could come from these twenty applicants and this was a chance for them to make their own judgements about who they may be compatible with.

In the end, ten of the applicants were offered places on course CCMO/15/13 and they all accepted. It was now just a case of sorting out the course fee. All ten successful candidates got a bursary from the Meteorological Office which went a substantial way to meeting the total cost. Eight candidates had sufficient funds of their own to meet the rest of the cost but the remaining two, including Bertram Gust, had to take out a loan with the Guild of Cloud Machine-Owners' to cover the remainder.

Learning to fly

Oscar left RAF Valley to make the journey to Bishops Court in Northern Ireland. He took the ferry from Holyhead to Dublin and then drove north. He headed for Downpatrick and from there to the old airfield at which the Training Centre had been established. On arrival he was directed to his accommodation. He had a surprise when he found that he would be living in a billet that had been constructed during the Second World War but outer appearances can be deceiving and, once inside, his initial anxiety evaporated. His room was ample in size and nicely decorated and furnished. He had his own washing facilities and toilet. The billet housed four individuals in the same fashion and they shared the facilities that were to be used for washing, drying and ironing clothes. Being on the main site of the old airfield, there was a dining hall and social club. Oscar had a feeling from the moment he arrived that he would be comfortable here.

Bertram's exit from Inverness was rather stormy. The amount of baggage he was loading into his car was more than would be required for a week's course and, suspicions aroused, his wife Morag checked the wardrobe and chest of drawers in their bedroom. Bertram was taking everything he owned. It was clear to Morag that her husband was jumping ship and she confronted him.

"Where do you think you are going?" she asked.

"I'm heading for a bagpipe free zone," he replied.

"Don't give me that. Tell me what you are doing."

"I'm leaving you Morag, you and your mother and father."

Before things started to get nasty, Bertram got rapidly into his car and he sped off. That was the last time he ever saw Morag or any other member of the MacCloud household.

The drive down to Stranraer was long and laborious and Bertram had time to reflect on what he had just done. He felt guilty about leaving Morag but he couldn't go on living with her parents any longer and his wife would not agree to look for alternatives. He had felt trapped but now there might be a chance for a fresh start.

The sea crossing to Larne passed quickly and then Bertram drove down to Downpatrick before heading for Bishops Court. On arrival he, like Oscar, was directed to his accommodation. The outside of his billet had no effect on him. At this moment in time, any place would be acceptable. It was a coincidence that Bertram and Oscar wound up in the same billet but they got on with each other famously from the start.

Soon after meeting up, the two aspiring cloud machine pilots met up with the rest of the successful course applicants in the dining hall and discovered that there would be ten of them in total. It didn't take long for everyone to get to know each other and they began to discuss the course they had all managed to get a place on.

The Training Centre social club was frequented by all the members of course CCMO/15/13 that evening and all had had a message to collect at the bar regarding where everything would start and at what time the next day. There was considerable excitement as to what was in store.

The course at Bishops Court was pretty intensive but each trainee found it totally fascinating. Getting to see a cloud machine for the first time was something in itself but getting on board and seeing the inside was a real experience. The machines at Bishops Court only differed in one way from those at Wythenshawe Weather Centre. They had an additional seat in the cockpit which was situated at the side of the pilot's position. This is where an instructor would be seated. Each trainee had his own personal instructor to take him through the whole course.

Getting to know the machine was first priority before a trainee got his first flight. It took all the trainees a little time to adjust to the fact that all the flying training was to be conducted at night when it was dark but the reasons for this were covered by their lessons on 'Air Law'. The first flights simply involved starting up the fan-duct motors, checking them and then getting airborne. Once airborne, the Identification Beacon was activated and they practised hovering. With all this completed they would contact ground control by radio and then land.

After the initial short flights above Bishops Court airfield the flights were extended a short distance to take the trainee pilots out over the Irish Sea. Although it was not the function of the pilot to make a cloud, a trainee needed to know what it was like to be in one and hence a flight engineer was aboard to fulfil that crewman's role. Several different types of cloud were manufactured to give trainees some experience but with the TV camera activated and the pop-up screen in front, at the pilot's eye level, visibility was not impaired and flying in a cloud was a bit of a buzz. Raining was quite good too but that had to be done before landing in the dark. It was important to remember to rain over the sea or the neighbours would complain. They got enough here as it was. Some of the trainees fell foul on this latter point and got a good dressing-down in the bargain.

Classroom work was essential in order to cover all the various things associated with flying, especially meteorology and air navigation. The former presented no difficulties for any of the course members but that was not so surprising considering that they all had a degree in the subject. Air navigation was another matter. Using the soakometer/navaid tended to make things easy. Punch in the latitude and longitude of your start and finish points; press the auto button and the cloud machine flew itself from where you were to where you wanted to go. Using the Plan Position

Indicator and chart was another matter and several air navigation exercises with and without the soakometer/navaid proved challenging.

The final subject studied on the course was concerned with Human Factors which covered things like keeping fit, sleep, sickness and when and when not to fly. Some of the trainees experienced only too well what it felt like to fly with a hangover and soon got familiar with the pilot's rule of thumb, 'twelve hours minimum between throttle and bottle'. One trainee fell foul of this commitment and was asked to leave the course, which was a salutary lesson for everyone.

Eventually a point was reached on the course when each trainee would be let loose with a cloud machine and a flight engineer for company. An exercise tested the crew's ability to make and deliver weather and the last hurdle that then remained was a set of exams to cover the subjects taught. Successful completion of all these qualified each course member to receive the coveted cloud pilot wings. It was a great pity that at such a late stage, one course member failed not only the exams but also the flight test with the result that only eight out of ten qualified.

A ceremony was held at Bishops Court outside the main hangar to award each new cloud pilot with his wings and Professor W.Flood from the Weather Making Research Centre at Llanbedr was guest of honour to make the awards, and families could attend.

The ceremony was held on a beautiful day and the famous Leyland Band provided some stirring brass band music to suit the occasion. It was of some relief to Bertram that Morag and the MacClouds had not attended and he was not jealous of his new friend Oscar, whose entire family seemed to be there. He was just glad that there had been no trouble.

Once the course was over, the eight new cloud pilots had the opportunity to visit the careers desk that had been set up in the Centre's main hall. Surprisingly, one of the newly qualified pilots made a quick exit, saying that he had lost interest in the weather, and disappeared off the scene. For the remaining seven there were nine jobs on offer, seven flying the research machines at Llanbedr and two at Wythenshawe. Henry Black and Larry Oliver manned the Wythenshawe desk and both spent a considerable time talking and explaining things to all the new pilots, but they hoped that Bertram and Oscar would be the ones joining them.

As the Wythenshawe duo explained, joining them had two distinct advantages. First, since there were not enough new pilots to go around, anyone joining them would probably end up doing work for the Weather Research Centre as well as the usual work that comes into Wythenshawe. And second, they were more likely to have a long term career at Wythenshawe than at Llanbedr since the Research Centre still had to prove its worth.

In the end, Larry and Henry were able to persuade their two favourites to join them by offering a part share in the cloud machines, Greystuff and Drip. At last, the two long- suffering flight engineers would be able to get airborne again and the thought of earning a wage again was cause for celebration.

New work at last

The day arrived when Henry finally teamed up officially with his new pilot, Bertram Gust, at Wythenshawe, and they sat down to talk about the future. The Weather Making Research Centre at Llanbedr had a requirement for two new pilots to further the work of two of its Faculties. They were prepared to sub-contract the work to a Wythenshawe crew on a temporary basis. The question for both of them was which Faculty they would prefer to work for.

When Bertram was shown around the Greystuff he was most impressed. It seemed hard to believe that he had a share in this cloud machine and his life seemed to have taken a leap forward from his marital, bagpipe ridden, home in Inverness. What a lot can happen in a short time, he thought.

Given that the Weather Making Research Centre had no cloud machines of their own at present, anyone entering into a sub-contract with them would have a free rein when it came to choosing a Faculty to work for. Henry, and his new colleague, looked carefully at the research each Faculty intended to carry out before making a choice. In the end, they chose the Faculty of Cloud Removal and an appointment was set up to meet its Head, Doctor Chris Blue.

Much the same thing happened with Larry and his new colleague, Oscar Blowhard. Having teamed up, the crew of the Drip got into serious discussion about the future, and much like the crew of the Greystuff, they thought that sub-contract work with the Weather Making Research

Centre offered the best chance to get some money flowing in. They too studied the work of each Faculty at Llanbedr but couldn't reach a decision. The work of two of the Faculties appealed to them: the Faculty of Wind and the Faculty of Special Effects and they made appointments to meet the heads of both before committing themselves.

Doctor Chris Blue was an amiable individual but it soon became apparent that he knew little about the weather or cloud machines. Henry wondered how he had got the job as Head of the Faculty but put his thoughts to one side for the moment. The research that the Faculty was to embark on was outlined, but the main aims being pursued were described as the universal removal of all types of cloud, and the establishment of the amount of water that needs to be maintained as water vapour permanently in the atmosphere. It all sounded a bit far fetched to Henry but if he was being paid to perform certain tasks, who was he to question the value of it. At the end of the meeting, Dr Blue posed the question, "Do you want the job?"

The crew of the Greystuff accepted the offer and heaved a sigh of relief in the knowledge that money would soon be coming in.

Larry and Bertram met Doctor Nott, the Head of the Faculty of Wind, and spent a considerable time discussing the aims that his Faculty would be pursuing, but were most put out when he announced that he had already appointed a crew to do the Faculty's work. Why take them through the rigmarole of an interview if there was nothing potentially for them at the end? Before their second interview took place with Doctor Whatsit, Head of the Faculty of Special Effects, they checked that a vacancy for a crew still existed. With an affirmative in that direction, they went ahead with the interview and discovered that the research that the Faculty would be doing was most interesting and they almost snatched the hand off the Faculty Head when he offered them the job.

One particular question that occurred to the two crews from Wythenshawe was where was the new research centre finding the cloud machine flight engineers to team up with the five new pilots that they had recruited? That was a mystery. Maybe in time they would get to know but for the moment it was just academic. The priority now was to get earning.

Help for a close friend

Cirrus was sitting in his Slaidburn home reading the Daily Gloom which didn't have much to interest him. Even his star didn't have anything to tell him that could brighten his day up. He lifted the paper away from his view as he heard Puffy arrive with his morning cup of coffee and immediately spotted his 'down in the mouth' demeanour.

"You're not looking very happy with yourself this morning, Puffy."

"I'm pretty fed up to tell you the truth skipper."

"Sit down and tell me what the problem is."

Evidently, the landlord renting the house to Puffy and his new wife Carol had decided that he wanted the property back and he had served notice on them.

"The problem is skipper, there is nowhere else in the village that we could rent and that means we will have to leave the area and I don't want to do that."

Cirrus was most upset to hear the plight of his flight engineer but on the spur of the moment he couldn't offer a solution.

"I'm very sorry to hear that Puffy but give me a bit of time and perhaps I might be able to come up with an idea."

For the moment, that's where things were left.

A couple of days later, Cirrus was having a conversation with Abigail at the Weather Centre just before she was about to set off on a job.

"Cirrus, why don't you offer them a room at your place until they find something?"

"I'm not really keen on that idea. I don't think it would help their marriage to be sleeping in the same house as me. Besides, I wouldn't want them to get too used to living with me; it might put them off trying to find another place."

"What about the old barn at the bottom of the garden? Could you not convert it into a place they could rent from you? That way, Puffy would still be on hand to do all the things he already does for you."

"That's a thought, but I would have to apply for planning permission, and then getting the job done may take quite a bit of time."

"Well, in that case why not give them a room on a temporary basis or get a small caravan for them and put that next to the barn?"

"Abigail, that's a cracking suggestion. They spend a lot of time apart as it is and when they are separated, Puffy stays in his old room at my place, so they wouldn't be spending too much time together in a caravan anyway."

"There you are then! Have a talk with Puffy and sound him out on the idea."

When Cirrus got into discussion with Puffy regarding his idea, Puffy jumped at it.

"That's great Captain. I'm sure Carol will feel the same. I'll tell her tonight."

"If she's ok with the idea, perhaps we could take a look at a caravan later this week," remarked Cirrus. "And I will contact an architect to draw up some plans to submit to the Local Council."

The next morning, Puffy was going about his work in the 'Aurora Cloudealis' in a jubilant fashion, whistling as he did so.

"I take it Carol was happy with our idea then Puffy?"

"Happy? Not likely! She's packed her bags and gone."

Cirrus was somewhat staggered by the news and confused by Puffy's apparent indifference about the situation.

"Why has she left you?"

"She said there was no way I was going to have her on the cheap. Living in a caravan was the last straw. She said it was hard enough me being married to you as well as her and if I expected her to live with me in a caravan I could go and take running jump."

The reference to Puffy being married to him made Cirrus feel a little uncomfortable, but before he could add anything, Puffy went on again.

"To tell you the truth skipper, it was not such a good idea marrying a girl so much younger than myself. We were two very different persons and she attracted a lot of attention from younger men, which I didn't like that much. So in a nutshell, I'm back!"

"Puffy, go and get that jug of 'Rob's Tea' and we'll celebrate together."

Teething Trouble

Henry and his new flight engineer, Bertram Gust, were attempting to familiarise themselves as a working crew aboard the Greystuff. Bertram had few hours of piloting cloud machines in his log book and needed to gain some more experience before carrying out any of the research work being planned by the Faculty of Cloud Removal. Henry had observed that Bertram had a tendency to be moody but couldn't find the right moment to approach him about the subject.

Morag, Bertram's wife, had felt betrayed when he left her and, encouraged by her mother, she had traced his whereabouts. From the moment she knew where he was she bombarded him with letters, texts, phone calls and emails, all of which were proving a little too much for him to handle and he took to the drink to drown out his depression. The drinking was not going to help his flying ability.

Things came to a head on a training flight aboard the Greystuff. The machine had got airborne, in the dark, at Llanbedr and flew a short distance to a position over Cardigan Bay before coming to a hover. Henry started the process of atomising water to create a cloud when Bertram announced that he must go the loo to relieve himself. That in itself was normal enough but he seemed to be away for an inordinately long time and when he started to shout that he had never used such a drafty loo before, Henry decided to investigate. He got out of his flight engineer's seat and made his way aft down the corridor that led to the stern of the machine and the toilet. As Henry reached the position that led to the exit door he turned and saw Bertram standing. He had opened the craft's exit door revealing the black mist outside and was relieving himself into their own Cumberland Grey, complaining at the same time how drafty it was. Once he had overcome his surprise, Henry persuaded his colleague to step back from the open door and return to the cockpit. He then pressed the button that closed the craft's door and, satisfied that it was closed properly, he went forard to join Bertram.

It was quite obvious that Bertram was inebriated but how he had hidden it from Henry was a mystery. The Greystuff remained hovering over Cardigan Bay for the next two hours whilst Henry plied his pilot with another kind of drink. This time, it was coffee and he continued until Bertram was sober enough to take command and then make rain before getting back to Llanbedr.

Henry had not foreseen this kind of problem but was made of pretty stern stuff. He had a long talk with Bertram after this incident and got to grips with the problem he was having to cope with. Being a man of the world, Henry sent Morag a letter and all communication between her and Bertram ceased from that moment on. Bertram never found out what Henry had said in the letter but whatever it was had worked and his drinking to excess came to an end. The Greystuff could now get on with the serious business of carrying out research and with luck, the only problems they would now have would be of a research nature.

# THE FIRST SNOW OF SUMMER

Thinking things through

What had happened to Puffy and his wife Carol had a big impact on Cirrus. He became more acutely aware of the age difference between Abigail and himself. More than anything, he did not want to be viewed as a dirty old man and that fact had been brought home to him both at the local pub and at Wythenshawe. It was not what people said to him directly, it was more the innuendo he overheard, but he knew what it all meant.

Cirrus was struggling with internal turmoil. On the one hand, part of him said that he should take the opportunity to have a loving relationship with Abigail and to hell with what people thought or said. It may be his last chance to love someone. On the other hand, he couldn't help wondering if he was taking advantage of the young woman in his life and she would come to regret it some time in the future. He would never forgive himself if that happened.

Trying to be realistic and sensitive about things, Cirrus decided that he would put the ring he bought into a secret place and leave it for now. Since Abigail had given no answer to his proposal he would leave things to take their natural course. There had been no impropriety involved and no harm done on that score. He did consider talking to Abigail about his feelings again but he decided that it was not appropriate. He had a duty to act as a respectable individual. Responsibility did however get in the way of emotion and that still caused him considerable pain.

Abigail noticed a slight change in the demeanour of Cirrus when she stayed with him in Slaidburn. She had half expected that he was going to propose to her again but it hadn't materialised. That didn't disappoint her too much; she was happy with the way things were. She was less than happy though about the way he seemed to have distanced himself from her lately and felt that a time was coming when she should 'clear the air', but she thought that that time had not yet arrived.

"Skipper, Mr Spite is on the phone for you."

"Thanks Puffy. Put him through."

"Morning Mr Spite. What can I do for you?"

"Cirrus I have received a rather unusual request and it's for something only you can do."

"You've got me intrigued. What is it?"

"It's a job for a TV Drama Company called Melodrama-in-Vision."

"I've heard of them. Are they the company that has been doing the detective series on Saturday nights?"

"That's the one. They are currently filming one of the series and it involves a bank robbery in Scarborough and they need our help."

"What exactly are they after?"

"They need heavy snow."

"Whatever for?"

"The robbery is supposed to take place in December and the robbers' getaway plan is foiled when it snows and the robbers get stuck, which allows the police to nab them."

"I can give them snow and plenty of it, but its July. Why don't they wait until December? By that time nature might supply them with the stuff free of charge."

"The company has a strict time schedule to keep to and that's why the programme must be recorded now. By the way, they could hardly leave it to nature to do the job. Nature is too unreliable."

"Don't they have machines that they can use to blow white stuff onto the set?"

"They do but as you know Scarborough is usually blessed with a sea breeze and it would blow the stuff away. Snow is a bit more adhesive and sticks better. More important than that is the fact that the prop is the whole of Scarborough and you couldn't blow white stuff all over that."

"I suppose you are right there."

After a little more 'to-ing and fro-ing', Cirrus accepted the job and took down a contact number for Melodrama-in-Vision.

"Snowing on Scarborough in July skipper! That's a bit iffy!"

"Well the company has all the necessary clearances to record the episode," replied Cirrus.

"But think about all them holidaymakers. They would be expecting to be on the beach putting sun tan lotion on, not shivering in snow. How long will it last?"

"I don't know how long it will take them to do the job. I will have to ring the company and ask them."

"How would the snow stick in July? I would have thought that the heat would just melt it all."

"It might. We will have to see. But if we go as an enormous Manchester Black, we could mask the whole of Scarborough from the sun and cool it right down, and if we dropped a huge quantity of heavy snow using large flakes then it should stick and last for some time."

"That might be so Captain but we will have to stay over the place for some time to keep it cool."

"Hello, this is the Melodrama-in-Vision Company. How can I help you?"

"This is Captain Cumulus. I am the skipper of the cloud machine Nimbus, that will be providing your snow in Scarborough later this month in connection with an episode you are making for your Saturday night TV detective series."

"Ah yes, I had heard that you would be doing it. How can I assist?"

"I want to speak to someone who can tell me the details of what you want me to do."

"I think I'd better put you through to the director."

"Who is the director?"

"Its Sir Archibald Godber. Just a moment and I will put you through."

"Hello Admiral, Sir Godber here. How can I help?"

Damn it! Not another Mr Vannin, thought Cirrus.

A long, rambling, conversation ensued, at the end of which Cirrus was not sure if he had got the information he needed or not.

"What's the score skipper?"

"I'm not sure that I can remember but I think it's like this: first, we arrive overhead Scarborough three days before the filming to cool the place down."

"That's going to make us popular."

"Filming will be on the twentieth of the month and hence we need to snow the day before and give a top up on the day itself. I am told that it should all be done in one day but we must be prepared to hang around in case they need another one or two."

"Blimey! It all sounds easy from our point of view but I hate to think how anyone taking a holiday that week is going to feel," commented Puffy.

A detective episode

The Alias gang were notorious gangsters in the TV series being shown on a weekly basis on Saturday nights and it was proving to be a great hit with viewers. After a period living the high life, villains, Bert Smith and Alf Jones, were running short of money. Holidays in the Caribbean with a string of good looking chicks don't come cheap and funds needed topping up. Bert and Alf were not small-time criminals. When they did a job it was big.

The story line goes that Bert and Alf went to Scarborough with some inside information regarding large payments in sterling being made into a certain bank in the town each week. That was important enough to warrant caging the place and a cheap and dingy room was rented that overlooked the bank that was receiving these weekly deposits. When a pattern had been observed, the duo set about finding out as much as they could about the internal details of the place and the working practice of the staff.

A plan was formulated to rob the bank at a time which was most advantageous to the TV criminals but it couldn't be done without a getaway car and a pre-planned escape route. An underworld driver was hired as part of the plot and after several rehearsals involving the robbers, police and innocent bystanders; everything was in place to do the shoot.

"Skipper, its Sir Gobchops on the phone from Melodrama-in-Vision."

"I'll take it in the lounge Puffy."

"Hello Sir Godber. What can I do for you?"

"We are ready to do the take on the next episode of 'Crime Winners' at Scarborough on the 21ˢᵗ of the month. This is just to let you know that you need to be overhead delivering a thick carpet of snow on both the 20ᵗʰ and the 21ˢᵗ and to be ready to remain on site if required. Is that clear to you Cumulus?"

Cirrus already knew that to make snow stick in the current heatwave would require blotting out the sun from Scarborough for three days before snowing otherwise the stuff would just melt away. To achieve a July carpet of snow it would take a full three days of overhead cloud cover before attempting it. The Nimbus would have to take on the form of a Manchester Black in order to be dark enough to prevent penetration by the sun's rays and this could be assisted by hovering over Scarborough at about five hundred feet.

"What about all the holidaymakers?" asked Puffy who went on: "Lots of people will have paid good money for a week in the sun by the sea. They won't be very happy about this skipper."

"Well nobody is going to tell them. At least they will get a good thriller to watch on TV in December."

The Nimbus was prepared for the film work on the 15ᵗʰ of the month at Wythenshawe and got airborne as darkness fell. A short flight was made to the Irish Sea, just west of Liverpool, and Puffy atomised the maximum water that he could in order to manufacture a menacingly large Manchester Black. Each of the saddle water tanks was filled to the brim and each refrigerator held as much ice as they could take. Once this was complete, the Nimbus headed east across country in the dark and no-one down below was aware of what was in store for somebody, somewhere.

The Pennines were crossed on the journey to Scarborough and on reaching the resort the Nimbus flew on to a point over the North Sea approximately ten nautical miles east of the town. Cirrus brought his cloud machine to a hover at five thousand feet and there he intended to stay until midnight. It was now 4-00am on the 16ᵗʰ and the Nimbus was well placed to lower the Scarborough temperature in due course.

July had been one of the best for weather that Scarborough had experienced for many years and folk had been flocking to the resort to enjoy the sun and sea air. Hoteliers and Guest Houses had not had such a good season for a long time and the current weather was making up for lost years. Ice cream, donkeys, candy floss and all those traditional seaside holiday treats were being enjoyed by a happy-looking throng, glad for a break from work. Children built castles in the sand whilst parents acted as labourers. No-one batted an eyelid about the Manchester Black hovering offshore. The wind was a westerly and was blowing the weather out to sea so there was no need to be concerned. The forecast was for continued sunshine for almost a full week. It should have been a grand week for a holiday.

On the 16th of July Scarborough was basking in floor to ceiling sunshine and the town was full to the brim with happy holiday makers. The beach was a patchwork quilt of human encampments made up of deck chairs and Li-Los. Grandmothers gave their pale legs an airing whilst granddads sported the latest headwear in the form of clean handkerchiefs. Mums and dads enjoyed their children whilst the older boys enjoyed the older girls. The sea was inviting but was freezing cold as usual, but that was no deterrent to youngsters or older boys chasing older girls. It was, without any doubt, a splendid day in Scarborough and it was being duly recorded on hundreds of postcards that would soon be on their way to greet those that were back at home, slaving away at work in the sweltering heat.

The day gave way to evening and whilst thousands walked along the promenade in the blissfully cool breeze, many others frequented the pubs and drank until it was time to go to their digs to sweat out the night and come up smelling the following day. Whilst all this was happening in Scarborough, ten miles offshore lay the Nimbus, hovering at five thousand feet. The crew were busy checking everything on board and casting glimpses of their destination on their TV screen.

Thirty minutes before midnight the Nimbus began moving towards Scarborough into a head wind that propelled nature's clouds in the opposite direction towards Holland, but no-one could see it in the dark. It took a full thirty minutes to get overhead Scarborough but when it did, the Nimbus was brought to a hover.

"Puffy, I'm going to take us down to five hundred feet and we will hover at that for the next three days."

"Very good Captain."

Slowly, the Manchester Black was lowered towards the holiday resort lying below them until it was only five hundred feet above it. At this height they would blot out the rising sun in the morning and for that matter, the next three days. The temperature would be nearer to that of winter a few hours after dawn. When a Manchester Black embraces any location it chooses to, it blots out light and prevents the sun's rays from having an impact, the result of which is a distinctly cold spell, and by 9-00am that's what Scarborough got.

"What a difference from yesterday!" said Mrs Whittaker staying at the 'Bowl-me-Over' guest house.

Her friend and companion, Elsie, replied, "And there's no sun today. It's almost night before its day."

Anyone who ventured out today in shorts and short-sleeved shirts or other forms of summer dress soon felt cold and retired to put something more appropriate on. No-one ventured on to the beach and the donkeys were left thinking about the toothpaste they hadn't used. Grandads with white hankies on their heads the previous day now sported mackintoshes and flat caps and spent most of the day in cafes reading newspapers. The day didn't get any better, but after a few drinks in the pub some began to forget what a dismal day it was.

On board the Nimbus it had been a fairly boring day but that was something that the crew had grown accustomed to over the years. Weather-making jobs often involve a lot of hovering around and so this was no different. Cirrus and Puffy always had a good stock of books around the Nimbus for just this kind of occasion. The beauty of the current situation was that they could sleep at the same time as everyone down below in Scarborough, which made a nice change. It should be pointed out, however, that not everyone on holiday in Scarborough had the same sleeping patterns as those onboard the Nimbus. Night time is when the older boys do more serious chasing of the older girls, but when you reach the age of Cirrus and Puffy it's best not to dwell too much on what goes on, especially when the older girls get caught by the older boys.

The 18th was the second day that the Nimbus practically sat on Scarborough and the second cold and dismal day was not having a good effect on the holidaymakers who now had to work on their imaginations as to what they could do to while away the time without it costing a fortune. Some, with children, had the hardest time, but they always do. How long can you endure squawking kids without doing something criminal? Fortunately, there were no reports of child murders but there was still time.

The turn in the weather was no problem to Mrs Whittaker and her friend Elsie staying in the 'Bowl-me-Over' guest house. They had been coming here for forty years and they had seen it all before. There was nothing that knitting couldn't cure and if you add a pot of tea to it, they could ignore everything just like their mothers had done during the wartime blitz on their hometown, Manchester.

The 19th brought a real downturn to everything. The first snow of summer fell on Scarborough and it was not well received. Thick flakes of it fell for hours on end and a carpet of white lay across the whole place. A bikini is no protection against a heavy snowfall and those that didn't know would do, by the end of the day. For many this was the last straw, or maybe that should be the last flake, and a number of holidaymakers started on an early holiday departure from snow-covered Scarborough.

"They don't tell you it snows in July at Scarborough in the holiday brochures do they?"

"No they don't and it's perishing cold!"

"Its Spain next year my Wilf says."

And so it went on as people struggled with their kids and their luggage to the railway station and bus terminal. The more affluent ones headed home in their cars but not before struggling with their kids and their luggage and in some cases with their wives or partners as well. The only ones that didn't mind struggling were the older boys with the older girls.

The exodus from Scarborough was not a complete exodus, for folks in this part of the world are pretty robust and the changing seasons were no surprise to many. The pubs were not quite as full during the evening but a degree of anticipation was finding its way around as news spread about the filming tomorrow of a bank robbery in a street called Westborough and it was all part of the popular Saturday night detective series called 'Crime Winners'.

Onboard the Nimbus, Cirrus was most pleased with the snow he had deposited on the resort and it appeared to be sticking well. His presence had prevented the sun from doing any warming but it would still be necessary to top things up in the early morning before filming got underway.

Sir Archibald Godber was most impressed with the job that the Nimbus had done and was all geared up to do the shoot on the 20th. The Alias gang would be filmed inside the bank, holding up the cashiers at gunpoint. The getaway car and accomplice driver would be waiting outside. The cameras and other equipment belonging to the 'Melodrama-in-Vision' company had been strategically placed to record the event from the best vantage points and the acting police officers were standing by to perform their film roles. The scene was well and truly set.

Whilst the Melodrama-in-Vision company was well satisfied with the set, the local Tourist Office was far from happy. They had had a lot of complaints about the weather, with many folks feeling angry that there was nothing in the brochures to prepare them for summer snow. It was hard enough trying to explain that the vagaries of the British weather were not down to the Tourist Board, but when it became common knowledge that the Local Authority had actually cleared the summer snow for filming by a TV drama company, it became downright dangerous. The Tourist board staff were threatened and abused and a number of holidaymakers demanded Compensation, which they were not in a position to give. The Tourist Board Office was shut at lunchtime on the 19th and the staff went into hiding.

An episode of 'Crime Winners'

The morning of the 20th finally arrived and with it another heavy fall of snow, care of the Nimbus. If any of the white stuff had melted during the night it was being replaced and fast. The exodus from Scarborough began again with a vengeance. There was a limit to what holidaymakers could endure in July and few wanted to purchase winter woollies in the middle of summer. The first snow of summer was certainly making an impact and the local police were having a job keeping the set clear of the throng rushing to the railway station.

The Manchester Black which had remained above the town at five hundred feet for the last three days stopped snowing mid-morning to allow filming to start. The first part of filming was not weather-dependent. The Alias gang, comprised of Bert Smith and Alf Jones, were busy pointing guns at the counter clerks inside the bank that had been chosen for the episode. In true gangster style, Bert and Joe issued a ream of instructions to the clerks to fill their sacks with all the money in the place and the clerks complied in a meekly fashion which is not usual in this part of the country.

Bert, using his mobile phone, signalled to the driver of the getaway car to make his way to the front of the bank to meet him. A final instruction was issued to the Bank clerks to lie down on the floor as they exited the now penniless establishment.

Fred Irony, the getaway car driver, started the engine up and released the handbrake in order to make his way speedily to the bank, which was just around the corner. As soon as he attempted to accelerate away, the car wheels started to spin in the deep snow and the back end went in a different direction to the front. Fred had tremendous difficulty trying to drive the short distance to the front of the bank where Bert and Alf stood outside the front door each holding several sacks of illgotten money. They looked left and right and then right and left but apart from scores of exiting holidaymakers there was no sign of Fred and the getaway car and that gave the Bank clerks ample opportunity to call the police.

In a terribly slow and erratic manner, the getaway car appeared in Westborough, the street in which the bank was situated, and the filming, now reaching its climax, attracted considerable interest amongst the escaping throng. Fred eventually skidded to a halt outside the bank to collect his two criminal colleagues. The sacks of money were stowed in the boot and the two robbers jumped in the car, removing their balaclavas at the same time.

"Where the hell have you been?"

"I had a hell of a job getting here at all in this bloody snow!"

Having exchanged pleasantries, the car sped off into a dangerous slide which took Fred to the limit of his driving skills to recover from and then they started into a second.

The skidding progress of the getaway car and the bank's money down Westborough was joined by an equally skidding police car that highlighted its presence with a blaring siren and flashing blue light. The police car made better progress than the getaway car for the local police drivers were better trained at coping with snow in summer. The two skidding vehicles performed a miraculous turn into Valley Bridge Road with the public watching the spectacle with glee. It was most unfortunate that the two vehicles could not stop turning and a crowd of folk had to scatter to allow the wall of the railway station to bring them to very dented halt. This proved to be a marvellous opportunity for the Alias gang to be arrested and a great cheer went up from the crowd who had temporarily forgotten about escaping and remembered the TV series 'Crime Winners'.

Sir Archibald Godber, the film director, was pleased with how the story line had worked: Two hapless robbers who had planned and executed a Bank robbery in the middle of winter had made no allowance for inclement weather and they had got caught out.

'Wizzo!' thought Sir Godber.

The director was, however, a perfectionist and felt that one or two minor things could be improved on and decided that a further shoot would be required on the 21st.

Word of another shoot got around fast and before Sir Godber and his crew could exit the set they came under snowball attack. Northerners are a hardy lot but there is a limit to how much 'mucking about' they would take and they had reached their summer snow limit. Two snowballs to the back of the head brought the required results and Sir Godber capitulated and then sneezed before announcing that his team would use what was already in the can.

Cirrus was delighted to be told that his services were no longer required and he lifted the Nimbus to five thousand feet before making his way back to a position over the North Sea, ten miles east of Scarborough where he hovered. It was grand watching the snow melt and run away from that distance but not as nice close up. When it got dark he would rain and when he had got rid of his Manchester Black he would head back to Wythenshawe and a well-earned rest.

It only took a couple of days for Scarborough to get back to normal and when the newspapers spread the story of the first snow of summer, tourism got back to where it was before. Business boomed again although in the case of Mrs Whittaker and her friend Elsie it wouldn't have made a blind bit of difference.

In December, the latest episode of 'Crime Winners' featured on Saturday night TV titled 'Snow and Grab' and it was viewed by all those holidaying at the time in Scarborough. It was a great hit, just like the two skidding cars.

149

Affairs of the heart

It was great to be back in Slaidburn after snowing on Scarborough. This is a remarkably beautiful place at the best of times, thought Cirrus, but even more so in the sunshine. The livestock roaming the fields adding something, and the whole village with its old church, school, pub and houses had an air of tranquillity about it that warmed his heart. Sitting in his lounge with a cup of coffee and listening to Leyland Band playing some of the music composed by Lucy Pankhurst took him back to that wonderful concert they conducted on St.Kilda. He was at peace with the world and that feeling had been enhanced by his faithful engineer, Puffy, being back in the Aurora Cloudealis. With Puffy living in again, things were running nice and smoothly. It also made a difference having Abigail here for a few days and it was nice to gaze at her in the garden putting out some plants. She was a lovely young woman to look at and Cirrus found her very desirable. His feelings for her had not changed.

Abigail knew that Cirrus had fallen for her and she had the same feeling for him. The age difference didn't matter to her and indeed, she felt far more comfortable in the company of a mature adult than most of the young men she had had a relationship with. She was aware, however, that Cirrus was a bit more on his guard with her and she wanted to know why. She also knew that she would have to respond to his proposal with great care for she knew that Cirrus was a most sensitive person.

"Cirrus, I've been meaning to ask you something for some time."

"And what's that Abigail?"

"I've noticed lately that you have become... a little distanced from me and I can't help wondering why. Is it something I have done or said or not said?"

Cirrus had to pause before he answered and whilst he did so he decided that honesty would be the best policy.

"Abigail, it worries me tremendously that there is such a large age gap between us. I get a fair amount of ridicule about having a relationship with you and I suppose it's the same for you. I don't want you to be exposed to that."

"That doesn't bother me in the slightest. The enjoyment I get from being with you more than compensates for that."

That was music to the ears of Cirrus.

"You are young Abigail and I can't help wondering that if you make a commitment to me you may in the future wish you hadn't and that worries me too."

"Every couple run a risk of things not working out in the future but that's the risk everybody takes. I think you have been influenced too much by what happened to Puffy and Carol. They are two very different people from us, Cirrus."

"Yes, I have to agree with that."

"Look, if you are unsure what you would like to do next why not leave things as they are. We are enjoying each other as we are aren't we?"

"Yes we are."

"So why spoil things? I'm sure that time will resolve everything and I can wait, and I think I want to wait for now. I'm enjoying you as you are. Couldn't you tell?"

And there matters of love were left and it was marked with a passionate embrace.

THE GAWMA AWARDS

Relaxing at home

Captain Cirrus Cumulus was sitting in the lounge of his Slaidburn home, taking his morning coffee and contemplating on the plight of his country. It seemed to Cirrus that the Government had no intention of doing what the country thought it should be doing but before he could get his thoughts into some kind of perspective his faithful engineer, Puffy, entered the room.

"Morning skipper! Here's your morning coffee and the latest edition of the Monthly Downpour which the postman has just delivered."

"Thanks Puffy!"

Cirrus quickly scanned the journal which the Guild of Cloud-Owners' published. He was looking for a report on the job he had just completed at Scarborough. Being the first time that a cloud machine had produced snow in summer, he thought it would be worthy of a mention but he could find no reference to it. What did catch his attention was an announcement on page five.

GAWMA Awards

Each year The Guild of Cloud-Owners' gave awards for various achievements which it called GAWMA Awards (Guild's Annual Weather Making Awards). These awards were always made at a special ceremony held on St.Swithin's Day, July 15th in the Silver Lining Club at Wythenshawe

Weather Centre. This was an occasion which all cloud machine crews were expected to attend and medals would be worn. This was an event that Captain Cumulus and his Flight Engineer, Percival White, had not missed for many years and this year's event would be the first at which the Captain could wear his CDM.

The Guild had instituted a process of selection for the awards which invited all the cloud machine owners to nominate people for each one and then a panel of judges would make the final choice. The recipients would only get to know of their success on the night.

"Puffy, Puffy," shouted Cirrus.

"What's up skipper?" enquired Puffy.

"I need your help in making some nominations for this year's GAWMA Awards."

"Oh, the Gawmless Awards! Its that time of year again. Well I suppose we better go through the list like we usually do."

First on the list was the award for the 'Most Elegant Cloud' of the year, and both Cirrus and Puffy had to scratch their heads to come up with a nomination. After considerable deliberation they remembered the fund raising event that had been held at Llandudno. This took the form of a 'Who is the prettiest cloud' contest and there had been six contenders.

"Who were the six contenders Puffy? I can't remember."

"There was the Flier, the Dismal, the Spitting and Lucy Windrush in the Softly Blows."

"Oh yes! I remember now. The Softly Blows had blue tints in it."

Puffy continued. "I'm sure you will remember the next two. There was the all red Skylark and the multi-coloured Mohican, Astro."

"What a spectacle that was. Who was the winner?"

"Sunny Blue in the Flier won it."

"Then I think we should nominate the Flier for the award."

Thoughts now turned to the 'Most Unfortunate Incident' of the year award but this time, the crew of the Nimbus thought that they should be the recipients. The last twelve months had not been incident free. There had been the time they had crashed on the side of Snaefell in the Isle-of-Man and had been hospitalised. There was the time when the Nimbus had had a missile hit it in the nether regions whilst doing trials work for the Navy, and finally, there was the time they had frozen into a block of ice and landed on the top of a lighthouse near Wick in Scotland. In spite of all this they couldn't nominate themselves and so it was back to the drawing board.

They recalled the incident involving Lucy Windrush in the Softly Blows in which she drifted on the wind, natural and man made, for many days before crash-landing on the remote island of St.Kilda off the coast of the Hebridean Islands in Scotland. Then they recalled the sad incident in which the late Al Blighty had, met his end aboard the Greystuff on Blackpool Tower. They both agreed that Als untimely death was most unfortunate. On balance they agreed that the incident involving Lucy warranted their nomination.

The crew of the Nimbus took a short break before coming back to the nominations business.

"What's next?" asked Puffy.

"Next comes the 'Most Challenging Job' of the year award."

"Filling Lake Windermere was a big challenge skipper."

"So it was, but we can't nominate ourselves."

"The Great Cloud Parade was another big one."

Cirrus wished Puffy had not mentioned that. It had certainly been a challenge but he had not survived it without getting a reprimand for soaking the Queen and as far as he was concerned it was best forgotten and, for that matter, so was the filling of Lake Windermere. That had also not been free from problems although he had not been implicated.

"Puffy, I think Eddie Stormbart should be recognised for all the work he organises for the Government in connection with its Foreign Aid programme."

"Skipper, I think I agree with you on that. Those convoys to Africa and other places are helping to create fertile land on which crops can be grown and in countries in which starvation is a serious problem. Yes I agree with you. Nominate Eddie Stormbart."

'The Most Dangerous Job' of the year award posed its own special difficulties for the crew of the Nimbus. As hard as they tried, they could think of no-one more deserving of this award than themselves. It was the Nimbus that had led the team to fight fires in the Keilder forest. It was the Nimbus that had flown a spy into Perechyn in the Ukraine. It was the Nimbus that had guided the Glasson Voyager from mid Atlantic to

Barrow when it had lost all electrical power. No matter how hard they tried to think of a more deserving cloud machine, they kept coming back to the conclusion that the worthy recipients were the crew of the Nimbus. Since they could not nominate themselves they decided to leave this award nomination blank.

Four down, four to go

"Captain, this is getting a bit tedious now. How many more nominees must we put forward? I want to get on with some gardening."

"I know how you feel but try and remember that these awards are treasured by those who receive them. They are considered special since it's their colleagues who put them forward for it."

"How many more have we got to look at?"

"There are eight altogether and so far we have done four."

"So four to go," said a rather tiring Puffy. "Which comes next?"

"It's the 'Most Elegant Cloud Machine' of the year."

"That must be us again," replied Puffy. "That new Nimbus of ours looks pristine compared with all the others at Wythenshawe."

"But we haven't had it very long. I think we should be thinking of the most elegant machine for the majority of the year."

"In that case it must be the Drip. It hardly got used when Arthur owned it and even now that it belongs to his engineer, Larry Oliver, it doesn't get used much."

"That's a thought. Larry and his new pilot, Oscar Blowhard, are still under training at the Weather Making Research Centre at Llanbedr. I wonder how they are getting on."

"I've not heard a thing, skipper."

"Anyway, that sorts that one out. We will nominate the Drip."

"What's next?" asked Puffy, although it almost sounded like a demand rather than a question. He was clearly not as enthusiastic about this nomination business as his skipper."

"It's the 'Greatest Fund Raiser' of the year."

"Didn't Abigail raise the most with that 'who can glide the furthest' contest she held.

"You mean the one from the Isle-of-Man to Blackpool?"

"Yes, that's the one."

"It did raise a lot of money but I thought that Sunny Blue got more with his 'who is the prettiest cloud contest."

They both went into deep thought at this point but neither could be sure who had raised the most.

"Let's have a look in back copies of the Monthly Downpour. There's bound to be some figures in there."

Puffy rushed off to find the back copies, which he had a feeling were under the stuff that needed ironing. In fact he thought right now that he wished he was doing the ironing instead of this nominating stuff. Nevertheless he found the journals and took them back to his waiting skipper.

"Okey dokey, lets take a look through these and see what we can find out."

After a quarter of an hour they came across a report highlighting the huge success of the 'guess how long it will drizzle for' competition organised by Wally Lenticular. He had raised far more than Sunny or Abigail and it settled the outcome of who they would nominate.

"Righto then, it's Wally for nomination," and Puffy agreed.

The award for 'Best Backroom Boy' was a bit harder for Cirrus and Puffy to deal with. Apart from Mr Spite and his secretary, Goldilocks, they didn't have many dealings with the rest of the staff at Wythenshawe Weather Centre.

"I think we need to include the cleaning staff and the air traffic controllers in this one"

"It's a puzzler skipper but I would say that the Superintendent is a must and his secretary for that matter."

"Why Goldilocks?" asked Cirrus.

"Look how well she organised that debate about new EU rules. And, don't forget, she compiled the findings and duly forwarded them on. And it worked. What new rules have been made?"

"None to my knowledge!"

"Well there you are then."

"I still think that we shouldn't forget the cleaning staff. They keep the centre in tip-top condition."

"Who do we know?"

"What about Alice Clutterbuck? She's always in the hangar and you know how huge that is?"

"Alice! Now you come to mention it, I can picture her in my mind. She always has a sweeping brush in her hand."

"That's the one. She's always hard at it."

"What about the air traffic controllers? They do a splendid job getting us safely away from the Centre in-between all the traffic in and out of Manchester Airport."

"Yeah, you're right there skipper, but who do we know?"

"What's that bloke called that pops into the Silver Lining Club and only drinks water?"

"I think his name is Alec Burns."

"With a name like that he should be setting us on fire!"

"He got a safety award last year from the 'Eyeball Club'."

"Is that so? What is the eyeball club?"

"It's an association for air traffic controllers."

"Well bless me!"

After all that, the two Nimbus crew members decided that Mr Spite was head and shoulders above the rest and they decided to nominate him. The thing that had helped them reach this decision was the part Mr Spite had played in the funeral of Al Blighty. They much admired him for his compassion towards a colleague and that had settled the issue.

The last award requiring nominations was that for 'Best Crew' of the year and, taking everything that had been done in the year into account, the crew of the Nimbus came to the firm conclusion that they should be the recipients. Considering that they couldn't vote for themselves it placed them in another awkward position.

"In fairness Puffy, I think we should nominate someone else."

"That's fine skipper, but who?"

"I think Abigail and Josh in the Hurricane have done a lot of sterling work in the last twelve months."

"That might be so but she hasn't led an armada of clouds anywhere to do anything special. What about Wally and Bert in the Discovery?"

"I suppose that they too have had a busy year. Let's toss a coin to decide."

A coin was tossed and it was heads for Abigail and tails for Wally. The coin landed heads up.

With all the nominations out of the way there was time to think about something else, and soon the crew of the Nimbus got to talking about a return to Ballyhalbert. It would be great to get away but Puffy was a little concerned about Abigail. He didn't begrudge his skipper having a relationship with an attractive young woman but if she came to Northern Ireland with them he did not want to be a 'gooseberry'. For the moment he need not be concerned for Cirrus made no mention of his female friend.

St.Swithin's Day

At last July 15th had arrived and both crew members of the Nimbus strode into the vast hangar at Wythenshawe to be greeted by a most unusual sight. There must have been at least fifty cloud machines parked inside; twenty-five down each side. It was most rare indeed to see so many here at one time. The crews of each machine were all busy taking supplies on board their respective machines and preparing the drop-down double bunks on board. There was no accommodation available in the Weather Centre but that didn't matter since each crew could sleep aboard their own craft and have breakfast in it after a night of celebration. It was something of a legend that a number of years earlier, Snowy White in the Dismal had attempted to fly off just after the awards evening and took off, in his less than sober condition, into the flightpath of an incoming passenger jet on a flight from Glasgow to Manchester. The aircraft had to abort its landing to avoid a collision, and rumour has it that its Glaswegian passengers set a world record for the variety and intensity of the expletives they used.

The crew of the Nimbus bumped into lots of colleagues that they had not seen for some time and it was inevitable that they would spend time reminiscing. The business of setting up aboard their machine was put on the back burner until someone pointed out that they were cutting it fine.

One thing that did perturb Cirrus was the rumour that certain cloud owners had been busy canvassing colleagues for nominations. That was not what the awards were all about and it was hoped that the end results would not be influenced by this activity.

On entering the Silver Lining Club, Cirrus was spotted by Abigail and she made a beeline for him. She placed her arms inside both those of Cirrus and Puffy and the three of them walked proudly and happily into the main room. Cirrus felt particularly proud of the CDM that was getting an airing on the left lapel of his jacket, not to mention the good-looking young woman linking his right arm.

It seemed as if the whole weather making world were here tonight for the prestigious awards that were going to be made. Prudence McWhirter, Head-of-Care in the 'Head in the Sky' rest home in Grange-over-Sands was here along with the current residents.

The whole of the Wythenshawe Weather Centre staff were present including its Superintendent, Mr I.N.Spite CDM. There was staff from Black, Black & Blackemore's in deeper Salford who had manufactured every one of the machines currently parked in the hangar. The Guild of Cloud-Owners' had its own complement of individuals to swell the ranks. It was quite a gathering.

Having consulted the table plan, Abigail and the crew of the Nimbus made their way to the table they had been allocated. The whole organising had been done by Mr Spite's secretary, Goldilocks, although protocol demands that on this occasion she be referred to by her real name which is Miss Black. Cirrus gave her a nod of approval and a smile. She was too far away to give her anything else and, given her appearance in her low cut dress, Puffy would have loved to have done just that.

When the three happy weather-makers were seated they began to appreciate the sound of Leyland Brass Band who had recently returned from the European Championship in Oslo. They made a splendid sound and whilst listening, Cirrus spotted through the corner of his eye, the composer Lucy Pankhurst who Cirrus had commissioned to write pieces for brass in the past.

Momentarily the music stopped and as it did so another group of people entered the Club. To the amazement of Cirrus, Eddie Stormbart was amongst the new arrivals. This was most unusual; he was said to be one of the busiest men in Britain with all the convoy work he was involved with on behalf of the Government. The group arriving also included several important people from the University-of-Northern England's Department-of-Weather. Professor Flood, Head of the new Weather Making Research Centre in Llanbedr. Doctor Chris Blue, Head of the Faculty-of-Cloud Removal. Doctor Albert Whatsit, Head of the Faculty of Special Effects and finally, some of the Board-of-Directors of the new research facility, the most prominent of whom was Mr Oliver Hoodwink MP. There was no doubt that with all these high-flying top knobs present, this was going to be something very special.

When all seemed settled there was a shout from the back of the hall which resonated all around.

"Cirrus you old fart, where are you boyo?"

A rumble of laughter spread like wildfire.

"Skipper, it's that Welsh photographer, Elwyn."

Cirrus had been busy sinking into a low profile position and regretted the intervention by Puffy who proceeded to stand up and direct Elwyn to their table.

"Oh yacky daa, a spare seat. You don't mind if I join you boyos," said Elwyn as he made claim for the evening to the last remaining place in the hall.

"Ta for saving it for me Crimilus. I almost missed the awards. Dam good pint they serve yer."

Whilst the decorum of the evening had evaporated, Cirrus couldn't help being amused and looked forward to the proceedings that would soon get underway.

The awards ceremony

On each table there was a fine spread of food and drink, and as Leyland Band played, the gathering ate and drank in time which was quite impressive, especially when the Band played a march. By the time the presentations were to be made, the greater part of the audience were either exhausted or slightly inebriated.

The Band had stopped playing and a rather large and fierce looking man took centre-stage.

"Ladies, gentlemen and you lot. Please welcome the President of The Guild of Cloud- Owners', Mr George Fowlup."

A huge round of clapping accompanied the arrival of the Guild's President but it soon died down when he stepped forward to the microphone. He slowly took out of his pocket a wad of papers.

"I hope he's not going to read all that bloody lot boyo," remarked Elwyn.

Clearing his throat into the microphone resulted in the audience joining in but the noise all died down enough for the proceedings to begin.

"On behalf of The Guild of Cloud-Owners', allow me to welcome you all here at the Silver Lining Club on St.Swithin's Day for the Guild's Annual Weather Making Awards. You have all contributed to the selection of this years award winners and this has made it easy for the judges to reach a decision. Without further ado I will begin with tonight's awards."

A deathly silence descended on the proceedings as everyone awaited the results.

The ritual of throat clearing preceded the first announcement accompanied once more by the professional throat clearers amongst the gathering, and Elwyn was adept at doing it in Welsh.

"The first award of the evening will be for the 'Most Elegant Cloud of the Year." This was followed by a pause before the President continued.

"There were several nominations for this year's award and the top three were: Sunny Blue in the Flier, Albertino Insomnia in the Astro and finally, Lucy Windrush in the Softly Blows."

There were no real surprises here.

"Tonight's winner!"

Before the President got any further there was a roll on the drums.

"Tonight's winner for producing a beautiful pearly white Westmorland White cloud at the Cloud Beauty Contest held at Llandudno was........ Sunny Blue in the Flier."

A huge round of applause broke out as Sunny stepped onto the stage to receive his award which was a table lamp in the form of a Westmorland White cloud. There was no speech, just a thankyou, and Sunny stepped down to allow the President to continue.

The second award of the evening will be for the 'Most Elegant Machine of the Year', for which we received three nominations. They were the Nimbus, the Drip and the Skylark."

The nomination of the Skylark was a surprise and rumours suddenly flowed around the hall that its owner, Bill Jones, had canvassed for votes for several weeks prior to the presentations. The outcome could be problematical.

A roll of drums signalled that the winner was about to be announced and it was waited for eagerly.

This year's winner for maintaining their machine in pristine condition throughout the year is…….. Larry Oliver and his machine, the Drip.

There was a mixed reception to this announcement. On the one hand it was a relief that Bill Jones had not won. On the other, it seemed a little unfair that the Drip, which had spent a good deal of time doing nothing, had won. The Owner of the Drip, Larry Oliver, had however, taken what steps he could to get the machine back to weather- making and on balance this went down ok with those present.

"I thought there might have been a punch-up over that one boyo," remarked Elwyn but Cirrus refrained from commenting and proceedings moved on.

"The third award this evening will be for the 'Most Challenging Job of the Year' and out of several nominations the top three were the Nimbus, the Spitting and Mr Eddie Stormbart."

The announcement led to some incredulity that Windy Blower in Spitting had been nominated. It looked as if this was another blatant case of canvassing. In spite of this,it was something of a forgone conclusion as to who the winner was.

Another roll of drums signalled that the result was imminent.

"This year's winner for completing the 'Most Challenging Job of the Year' goes to…..

Mr Eddie Stormbart, for spearheading the convoys of Foreign Aid around the world, on behalf of the Government."

The audience stood and gave a resounding endorsement of the award as Eddie walked onto the stage, and again as he walked off.

Each award winner received an all glass trophy from the Guild, suitably engraved with the details of the recipient along with the year it was awarded. These awards were highly valued by both the winners and the losers. All the members of the Guild shared a desire to win one and have it in a prominent place in their home.

The President then went on: "The fourth award this evening is for the 'Greatest Fund Raiser of the Year' for which a number of nominations were received. The top three nominations were: First, Wally Lenticular for his excellent drizzle in his Discovery. Second, Sunny Blue for being the prettiest cloud in the Flier."

A huge number of wolf whistles at this point drowned out the President but they soon died out to allow him to continue.

"The third nomination was for Abigail Windrush." He couldn't get any further than that because of the fresh breakout of wolf whistles which continued for some time.

"The third nomination is for Abigail's triumph at gliding more accurately than anyone else."

"We all knew she was a high flier!" shouted someone from the audience but the unflinching President continued after a suitable drum roll.

"This years winner is Wally Lenticular for his first rate drizzle."

The result was greeted with a mixture of clapping and booing but it was all good natured and Wally was most pleased to step on to the stage to collect his Guild glass trophy and he was cheered as he left holding it aloft so that everyone could see it.

"We move on now to the fifth award and that is for the 'Most Unfortunate Incident of the Year', and I must say that there were an enormous number of nominations for this but we did narrow it down to the following: First the Nimbus for its crash on Snaefell, second, the Softly Blows for its long flight and eventual crash on the island of St.Kilda and finally, the Greystuff for its demise on Blackpool Tower.

"Admiral, I think you stand a good chance at this one boyo," remarked Elwyn.

A fresh drum roll drowned out Elwyn's next comment, which was a relief to Cirrus.

"This year's winner is Lucy Windrush in the Softly Blows."

There was a loud cheer as Lucy stepped onto the stage and the Band struck up the piece that her friend Lucy Pankhurst had composed for her – St.Kilda's Fling. And many of the audience drank in step with the lively music but not in tune.

Armed with her trophy, Lucy returned to her table to rejoin the man in her life, a certain Flight Lieutenant W.Waffler.

"I now move on to the sixth award which is the 'Backroom Boy of the Year' award. The top three nominations are as follows: first Miss Joanne Black for all her support work here at Wythenshawe."

Huge cheers interrupted proceedings and Puffy remarked that he never knew that Joanne was Goldilocks' first name.

"You learn something new every day," replied Cirrus.

"I go for weeks sometimes without learning anything boyos."

"The second nomination is the Superintendent here at Wythenshawe, Mr Ivor Spite, CDM."

A most dignified clapping accompanied the announcement along with a number of 'hear, hears!'. Ivor Spite CDM was held in high esteem by his colleagues.

"If I keep learning a lot of new things I'm going to have a bloody headache boyo."

"The third nomination is Prudence McWhirter for her outstanding work at the Guild's rest home, 'Head in the Sky' at Grange-over-Sands."

Another drum roll preceded the announcement of the winner.

"This year's winner is................ Prudence Mcwhirter."

Prudence got the second standing ovation of the evening and appeared most humble as she stepped on the stage to collect her award.

Tension began to build as the time arrived for the last two awards of the year to be announced, for they were generally regarded as the most prestigious. The President paused to allow everyone to get more drinks in and that didn't take long. The bar already had the details of what everyone wanted and an army of stewards flashed around the place with trays full of a great assortment of liquids. With suitable refreshments served things began again.

"The seventh award this evening will be the 'Most Dangerous Job of the Year' award.

The judges selected three of the nominations for this award for further consideration and they are as follows: first the Nimbus, second the Stormlark."

"What the hell did the Stormlark do?" asked Cirrus.

"He probably did a lot of canvassing skipper," replied Puffy.

"The third nomination is the Dismal."

There was something of surprise hush about the hall for no-one could work out what justified the choice of the Stormlark or the Dismal except their respective skippers and they were saying nothing.

A drum roll broke the mounting tension.

"This year's winner is the Nimbus and her skipper Cirrus Cumulus for his flight to the Ukraine with a Government official."

Everyone knew what that meant and a great applause broke out and continued as he walked on to the stage to collect his trophy. He had intended to speak into the microphone to say that he had not been alone on the mission but before he could he was turned around by a burly pair of arms and told politely but firmly where the exit was.

Abigail was the first to congratulate Cirrus on his return and did so with a loving kiss.

"Yachy da and well done boyo, but don't expect a kiss from me," commented Elwyn.

Cirrus wanted to celebrate there and then but there was still one more award and everybody was waiting to hear who had won it.

The final award for this year and the eighth of the evening is the 'Best Crew of the Year' award. The three nominations selected by the judges are as follows: first Cirrus Cumulus and Percival White in the Nimbus."

There was huge applause when this nomination was announced and Cirrus was embarrassed but thrilled at the apparent support he had from his Wythenshawe colleagues.

"The second nomination is Abigail Windrush and Josh Harrop in the Hurricane."

"Two bloody nominations on the same table. That's really something boyos," remarked Elwyn.

"The third and last nomination is that of Snowy White and Fred Hartshorn in the Dismal."

A hushed hall greeted this last nomination for no-one could work out why anyone would nominate Snowy. No-one could think of anything he and Fred had done to warrant nomination.

A drum roll got the attention of an anticipatory throng and the President was about to end their agonising anticipation.

"The winner of the 'Best Crew of the Year' Award.................is the crew of the Dismal, Snowy White and his engineer Fred Hartshorn."

Once the disbelief had settled in, a round of booing began as a precursor to the throwing of sugar lumps at the President. George Fowlup CDM proved to be most skilful at dodging sugar lumps but the thought of chairs impacted on his level of bravery and waving a white handkerchief, he made a rapid departure to somewhere behind the stage.

Snowy and Fred could be seen nowhere in the hall. It looked as if they had beaten a hasty retreat.

"Cirrus, you have been robbed of a well deserved award," said one of his colleagues.

"Never mind boyo. You're not exactly like the rest of your colleagues are you?"

"What do you mean by that?"

"You're not going home gawmless are you boyo?"

Before Cirrus could answer, Elwyn stretched his arm under the table and brought from under it a large brown envelope.

"There you are boyo. A 2014 Welsh Tourism Board Calendar Yachy da."

Cirrus was a little taken aback by this gesture and didn't notice the couple approaching his table as he looked at the calendar.

"Hello Captain Cumulus."

Cirrus looked up and was most surprised and delighted to see the two undergraduates that he and Wally Lenticular had provided work experience for to produce the calendar he presently held in his hands.

"Well bless me if it's not Sarah Whittle and John Davies! It's lovely to see you both but how did you get here?"

"Mr Lenticular invited us."

A long conversation ensued between Cirrus, Puffy, Abigail and the two undergraduates, and Elwyn drank through it all sinking further under the table as he did so. When the conversation reached its conclusion the question was asked as to where the Welsh photographer had gone, but the cleaners found him in the morning.

Bidding goodbye to their mentors, Sarah and John left arm in arm and Cirrus was rather taken by this. When he left the hall it was arm in arm with Abigail and the two of them enjoyed the feeling, and Puffy walking behind them could tell.

It seemed strange sauntering in to Wythenshawe's huge hangar to go to bed but they were not alone on this evening. A whole host of cloud machine crews were doing the same. Cirrus escorted Abigail to her night's abode, the Hurricane, and the two embraced before coming up for air and going their separate ways.

It had been a memorable night after a memorable year and the chances of it being any different in the next twelve months were not very likely, thought Cirrus. He boarded the Nimbus and made his way to the cockpit to join his faithful engineer, Puffy, and was greeted with a question.

"When are you going to marry that girl skipper?"

EPILOGUE

From its early beginnings the business of weather-making has come a long way. From the early days of 'one cloud fits all' to the current 'anything is possible' has been traced with the help of those 'in at the start'. The journey has been eventful in many ways.

Nothing in this world stands still and that is as true for weather-making as anything else. The establishment of a weather-making research centre may bode well for the future and developments are waited for with great anticipation. Whether man can control the weather remains to be seen but with the aid of entrepreneurs like Mr Vannin, anything seems possible.

Weather for social purposes has great potential and if it could be guaranteed, it would surely be both a boon to society and a huge money earner, providing it is not over- regulated by such bodies as the EU. It would, nevertheless, be an idea to create some kind of operating framework if only to prevent weather from being used for industrial sabotage.

Love has something in common with the weather. It blows hot and cold and that, to a degree, is true of Cirrus Cumulus and Abigail Windrush. Apart from the fact that the weather keeps them apart for long periods of time, they both, currently, lack the courage to take things to the next natural stage. There has not been a storm in their lives but neither has there been a sunny lining and if you are like me, you will be waiting for a sign in the sky.

ABOUT THE AUTHOR

This is the third book on weather making by the author, the first being – 'Making Rain and Other Things Is Our Business!' and the second – 'A Cloud's Life'.

Tony Smith is a retired Further Education Lecturer and former RAFVR(T) and SCC RNR Officer. He has a wealth of experience of young people and all things flying. As a Bachelor of Education and glider pilot, he is suitably qualified to waffle on about a lot of things.

When Tony's head is not in the clouds he builds model aircraft and helps a local Brass band.

Tony is married and has two daughters, two granddaughters and a grandson. He lives in Atherton, a former mining and mill town in the North West of England.

The Author and his daughter Hayley
Exploring ideas for shooting down clouds.

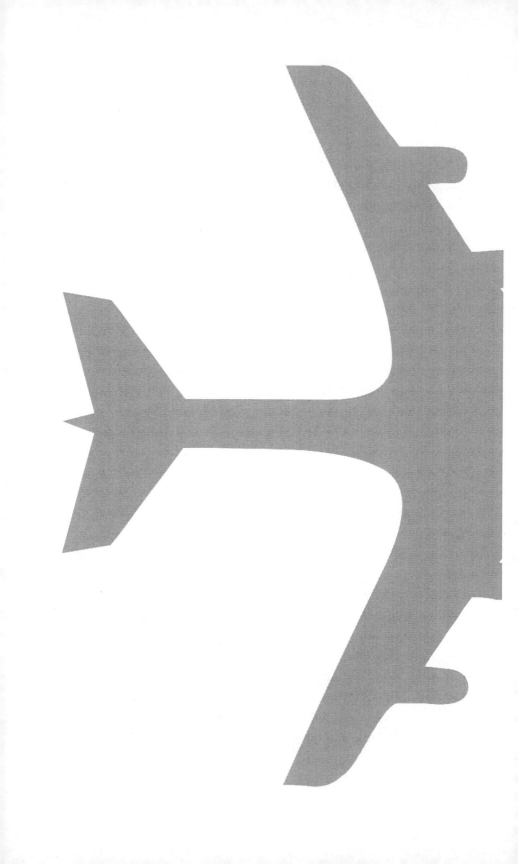

ILLUSTRATIONS

Illustration one

SIDE ELEVATION

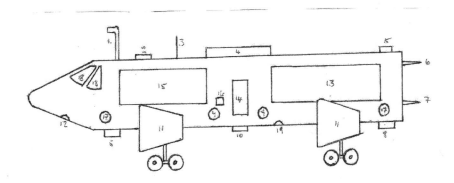

1. Periscope with tv camera which has infra-red capability to see through cloud or in the dark.
2. GPS antennae (Global Positioning System).
3. VSI antennae (Vertical Separation Indicator – used in cloud formation flying).
4. Emergency parachutes.
5. Identification Beacon (every cloud machine has its own ID code)
6. Telephone antennae.
7. Radio Transmitter/Receiver antennae.
8. Atomiser – converts water into cloud by a process of evaporation (some water is stored onboard, some as ice).
9. Dispenser – converts stored water and stored ice plus cloud vapour into rain by a process of melting and condensing.
10. SOAKometer – early form of navigation aid with built in water location system.
11. Fan Duct Motor – propels cloud. A cloud has its own natural buoyancy.
12. Porthole for winch cable.
13. Saddle type water storage tank.
14. Side entry door.
15. Fuel tank for Fan Duct Motors.
16. Panel of buttons to open/close entry door and deploy/retract entry ladders.
17. Loudpeakers.
18. Cockpit window.
19. Fuel hose point.

Illustration two

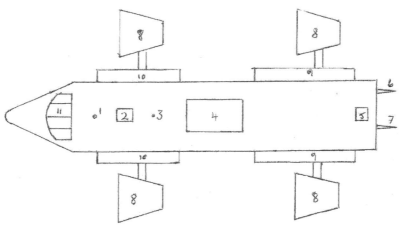

Direction of movement of Fan Duct Motors
to yaw the cloud left or right.
Movement made by cockpit rudder pedals.

1. Periscope with tv camera which has infra-red capability to see through cloud or in the dark.
2. GPS antennae (Global Positioning System).
3. VSI antennae (Vertical Separation Indicator – used in cloud formation flying).
4. Emergency parachutes.
5. Identification Beacon (every cloud machine has its own ID code)
6. Telephone antennae.
7. Radio Transmitter/Receiver antennae.
8. Fan Duct Motor – propels cloud. A cloud has its own natural buoyancy.
9. Saddle type water storage tank..
10. Fuel tank for Fan Duct Motors.
11. Cockpit window.

Illustration three

Manufacturers – Black, Black & Blackemore's, Salford

Cloud Machine – Nimbus – grade 1

FRONT VIEW

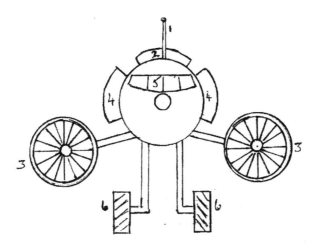

1. Periscope with tv camera which has infra-red capability to see through cloud or in the dark.
2. Emergency parachutes.
3. Fan Duct Motor – propels cloud. A cloud has its own natural buoyancy.
4. Fuel tank for Fan Duct Motors.
5. Cockpit window.
6. Rugged undercarriage.

Illustration four

Manufacturers – Black, Black & Blackemore's, Salford

Cloud Machine – Nimbus – grade 1

GENERAL ARRANGEMENTS

Fan Duct Motors (port side shown)

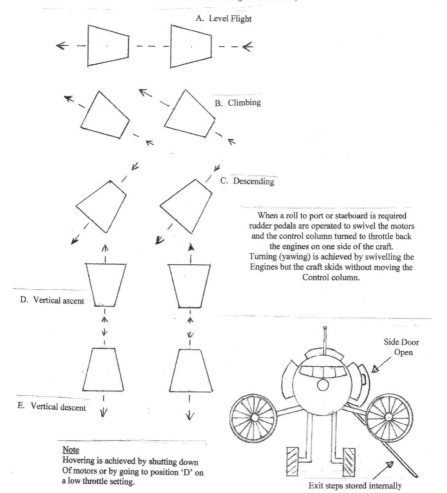

A. Level Flight

B. Climbing

C. Descending

When a roll to port or starboard is required
rudder pedals are operated to swivel the motors
and the control column turned to throttle back
the engines on one side of the craft.
Turning (yawing) is achieved by swivelling the
Engines but the craft skids without moving the
Control column.

D. Vertical ascent

E. Vertical descent

Side Door
Open

Note
Hovering is achieved by shutting down
Of motors or by going to position 'D' on
a low throttle setting.

Exit steps stored internally

Illustration five

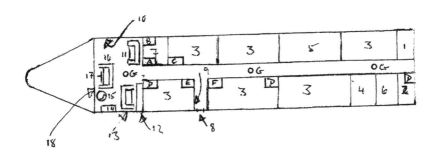

Emergency features

A First Aid Kit
B Fire Blanket
C Oxygen Masks
D Fire Extinguishers
E Parachutes
F Life Jackets
G Smoke Detectors

1. Wash room
2. Toilet
3. Refrigerator
4. Mixer
5. Sublimator
6. Van de Graaf Generator
7. Galley
8. Side entry door
9. Panel of buttons (includes door opening, access ladders & door jettison)
10. Drop-down bunk location
11. Passenger seat
12. Flight Engineer's station
13. Flight Engineer's seat
14. Winch winding mechanism
15. Plan Position Indicator
16. Pilot's seat
17. Control column
18. Flight deck instrument panel

Illustration six

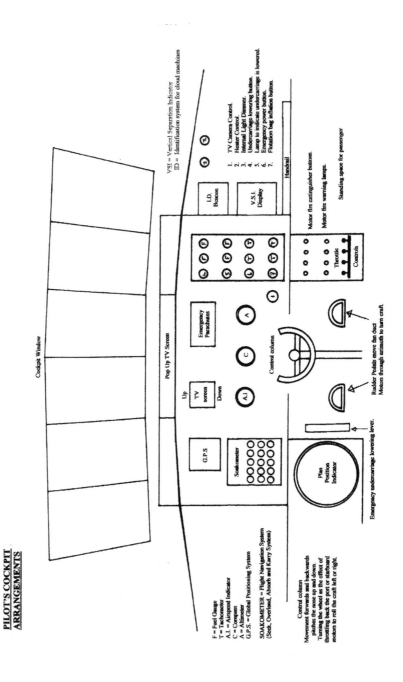

Cloud Machine – Nimbus – grade 1

Manufacturers – Black, Black & Blackemore's, Salford

PILOT'S COCKPIT
ARRANGEMENTS

Cockpit Window

F = Fuel Gauge
T = Tachometer
A.I. = Airspeed Indicator
C = Compass
A = Altimeter
G.P.S. = Global Positioning System

SOAKOMETER = Flight Navigation System
(Seek, Overland, Absorb and Karry System)

Control column
Movement forwards and backwards
pitches the nose up and down.
Turning the wheel as the effect of
throttling back the port or starboard
motors to roll the craft left or right.

G.P.S

Soakometer

Up
TV
screen
Down

A.I.

Emergency
Parachutes

Pop Up TV Screen

A

C

Control column

Plan
Position
Indicator

Emergency undercarriage lowering lever.

I.D.
Beacon

V.S.I.
Display

F

T

A

C

I

Motor fire extinguisher buttons.

Motor fire warning lamps.

Standing space for passenger

Throttle

Controls

Handrail

Rudder Pedals move fan duct
Motors through azimuth to turn craft.

VSI = Vertical Separation Indicator
ID = Identification system for cloud machines

1. TV Camera Control.
2. Heater Control.
3. Internal Light Dimmer.
4. Undercarriage lowering button.
5. Lamp to indicate undercarriage is lowered.
6. Emergency power button.
7. Flotation bag inflation button.

Illustration seven

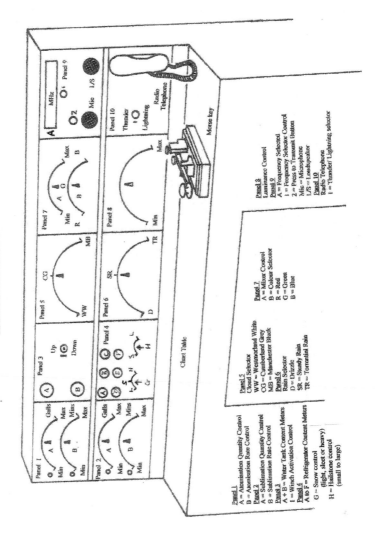

Cloud Machine – Nimbus – grade 1

Manufacturers – Black, Black & Blackmore's, Salford

Flight Engineers Station

Panel 1
A = Atomisation Quantity Control
B = Atomisation Rate Control
Panel 2
A = Sublimation Quantity Control
B = Sublimation Rate Control
Panel 3
A + B = Water Tank Content Meters
I = Winch Activation Control
Panel 4
A to F = Refrigerator Content Meters
G = Snow control
   (light, sleet or heavy)
H = Hailstone control
   (small to large)

Panel 5
Cloud Selector
WW = Westmorland White
CG = Cumberland Grey
MB = Manchester Black
Panel 6
Rain Selector
D = Drizzle
SR = Steady Rain
TR = Torrential Rain

Panel 7
A = Mixer Control
B = Colour Selector
R = Red
G = Green
B = Blue

Panel 8
Luminance Control
Panel 9
A = Frequency Selected
1 = Frequency Selector Control
2 = Press to Transmit Button
Mic = Microphone
L/S = Loudspeaker
Panel 10
Radio Telephone
1 = Thunder/ Lightning selector

MAPS

Map one

Locations of Fund Raising Events

England	
Scotland	
Isle-of-Man	
Morecambe Bay	
Isle-of-Anglesey	
Irish Sea	

1. Stranraer
2. Grange-over-Sands
3. Morecambe
4. Fleetwood
5. Douglas
6. Blackpool
7. Southport
8. New Brighton
9. Rhyl
10. Llandudno